Todd went silent for a moment.

"Wait, what's going on?" he asked. "Are you okay?"

"Yeah!" she blurted out too eagerly. "I mean, yes. I'm good. Why?"

"Because you sound strange. Like something's bothering you."

Just tell him...

Elle stood and began pacing the floor. "I, um...I received a weird phone call today. Voice mail, actually. Someone called me anonymously and I didn't pick up. So they left a message."

"Okay... What did the message say?"

"That they know what I'm doing. And if I don't stop, I won't make it out of the next attack alive."

Todd grunted into the phone. "The next attack? What the hell is that supposed to mean?"

"That whoever called had something to do with the crash at the forest preserve, and they're planning the next move against me." Elle's legs trembled uncontrollably. She stumbled over to her vanity and slumped down onto the white wooden stool.

BACKCOUNTRY COVER-UP

DENISE N. WHEATLEY

This book is dedicated to you, the readers! Thank you for coming along on yet another suspenseful journey with me. Keep sleuthing, friends!

HARLEQUIN®
INTRIGUE™

ISBN-13: 978-1-335-58233-1

Backcountry Cover-Up

Copyright © 2022 by Denise N. Wheatley

For questions and comments about the quality of this book, please contact us at CustomerService@Harlequin.com.

Harlequin Enterprises ULC
22 Adelaide St. West, 41st Floor
Toronto, Ontario M5H 4E3, Canada
www.Harlequin.com

Printed in U.S.A.

Recycling programs for this product may not exist in your area.

Denise N. Wheatley loves happy endings and the art of storytelling. Her novels run the romance gamut, and she strives to pen entertaining books that embody matters of the heart. She's an RWA member and holds a BA in English from the University of Illinois. When Denise isn't writing, she enjoys watching true crime TV and chatting with readers. Follow her on social media.

Instagram: @Denise_Wheatley_Writer
Twitter: @DeniseWheatley
BookBub: @DeniseNWheatley
Goodreads: Denise N. Wheatley

Books by Denise N. Wheatley

Harlequin Intrigue

Cold Case True Crime
Bayou Christmas Disappearance
The Heart-Shaped Murders
Backcountry Cover-Up

Visit the Author Profile page at Harlequin.com.

CAST OF CHARACTERS

Elle Scott—A highly regarded private investigator who is looking into the murder of her best friend.

Todd Jacobson—A former US marine turned deputy sheriff who's investigating his sister's murder.

Taylor Jacobson-Hendrix—Elle's best friend and Todd's sister who turns up dead after becoming a member of The Precious Jewels women's group.

Bryce Hendrix—Taylor's suspicious husband.

Rachel Bennet—Elle and Taylor's old high school friend and Taylor's confidant.

Chloe Hale—Taylor's protégée who she recruited into The Precious Jewels.

Sloane Whitlock—The founder of The Precious Jewels.

Bernard Glover—The chief deputy sheriff in Bradford, North Carolina.

Sara Ross—A hostile member of The Precious Jewels.

Audrey Bingham—Taylor's friend and business partner.

Chapter One

Elle Scott dug her fingernails into the steering wheel of her rented silver sedan. She made a sharp right turn, slamming on the brakes as her car skidded over River Birch Park's rocky terrain.

Dusk had fallen over her hometown of Bradford, North Carolina. Gone was the afternoon's bright blue sky. It had transformed into a sea of pinkish gray mist. The low-hanging sun was fading behind a curtain of clouds. That had been Elle's cue to pack up and head back to her parents' house.

A stinging chill crawled along the private investigator's skin. She inhaled slowly, waiting for her breathing to stabilize.

She had just left the crime scene where her best friend, Taylor Jacobson-Hendrix, had been found dead. Taylor's brother, Todd, was the one who'd called Elle a week prior to break the news.

"Taylor is gone," he'd whispered so faintly that she asked him to repeat himself.

"Gone? What do you mean, *gone*? Did she finally run off and leave her husband?"

"No, Elle. She—she's dead."

The words had numbed her limbs and sent her crashing to the floor of her Manhattan apartment. She'd remained there for almost an hour. Todd stayed on the phone with her the whole time. He explained how a park ranger had spotted Taylor's lifeless body lying underneath a massive tulip tree along River Birch Park's running trail.

The coroner ruled her death an accident, blaming her broken neck on a fall caused by the path's jagged ground.

Todd didn't believe it. Neither did Elle.

Taylor could've jogged the park's trail blindfolded. She'd been running it for years. It had been her and Elle's personal track all throughout high school and college. When Elle moved away ten years ago, Taylor continued to utilize it religiously.

Todd was infuriated when the sheriff's department stood by the medical examiner's ruling and closed the case. As a former US marine turned deputy sheriff in training, he felt betrayed by his hometown's law enforcement agency. Todd was convinced that his sister's death involved foul play. He'd begged the sheriff to further investigate the case, but his pleas had gone unanswered.

So he'd turned to Elle, asking that she bump up her plans to return home for the holidays and help him investigate Taylor's death. She'd booked the first flight out.

What really happened to you, Taylor?

A pair of blinding headlights flashed through Elle's back windshield. She peered into the rearview mirror. A black pickup truck was tailgating her down the park's gritty, sloped road.

"Could you back up, please?" Elle grumbled just as her cell phone rang.

Todd's name flashed across the screen, along with the photo of him and Taylor she'd saved under his contact information.

Her chest pulled at the sight. Todd and Taylor had taken the picture last year at the Marine Corps birthday ball.

Taylor's bright, wide-set eyes and signature crooked grin jumped off the screen. She and Todd had their arms wrapped securely around each other, which was how they'd always posed for photos considering how close they were.

Todd's crisp blue uniform was pressed to perfection. He could've passed for a young Blair Underwood with his dark, closely cropped hair, perfectly trimmed mustache, deep brown skin and smile so radiant it could light up a movie set.

Elle had had the biggest crush on Todd when they were younger. But she'd admired him from afar, figuring that he saw her as nothing more than his little sister's bestie. Eventually he'd enlisted in the military and she'd moved away, furthering the gap between them.

Taylor had acted as their liaison through the years, keeping them posted on what the other was up to from time to time.

And now she was gone.

Who knew I'd end up reconnecting with your brother through your death...

Elle's cell phone rang for a third time. She snapped out of her thoughts and tapped the steering wheel's Bluetooth button.

"Hey, Todd."

"Hey, just checking in. How are things going?"

His smooth, deep voice flowed through the speakers. It managed to relax her tense shoulders as she melted into the seat.

"I was just thinking about you," she said. "I'm actually leaving River Birch Park now."

"Really? You were out there for a long time. Sorry I couldn't join you. My weapons use training class went way over. But please tell me that you found some sort of evidence that we can work with. *Anything.*"

Elle's lips twisted in defeat. "Unfortunately, I didn't. And I scoured every inch of the area where Taylor's body was found. The only reason I left is because it started getting dark and I forgot to pack my flashlight. But I was confident that I'd find something. I guess I should've added crime scene investigation tactics to my forensic accounting and surveillance techniques studies."

"Look, don't underestimate your capabilities, Elle. I trust your investigative skills. You are truly gifted. I'm convinced that together, you and I are going to solve this case."

"Thanks, Todd. I appreciate your faith in me."

Elle slowed down when she reached the bottom of the road. The pickup truck that had been trailing her came to a screeching halt inches away from her bumper. The driver pressed down on the horn.

"Oh, come on!" Elle yelled, craning her neck toward the side-view mirror.

The truck's windows were tinted. All she could make out was the middle finger being flipped at her.

Elle waved the driver off. *"Jerk!"*

"What is going on out there?" Todd asked.

"Some jackass has been tailgating me ever since I left the crime scene. Now they're mad because I won't jet off into the intersection and get hit by oncoming traffic."

"I can't stand road ragers. Where exactly are you?"

"At the corner of Birch Street and Livingston Avenue." Elle looked to her right, then left. "The roads are jam-packed. Is there some sort of special event happening tonight?"

"Yep. The Christmas parade. I'm sure everybody is making their way downtown now. The main thoroughfare is gonna be flooded with holiday floats, sleighs, horse-drawn carriages, the whole nine."

"Ugh. I used to love Bradford's Christmas parade. But tonight, I couldn't be in a less festive mood. I have got to get out of here. I need to take a detour—"

Bee-ep!

Elle jumped in her seat as the pickup truck's shrill horn blared behind her.

"All right, all right!" she yelled.

"Listen, why don't you cut through the Everest Forest Preserve? That'll get you back to your parents' house pretty quickly." Todd paused. "Better yet, why don't we meet up for a drink? Sounds like you could use one. I know I could."

"After the day I've had?" Elle replied. "I could definitely go for a nice strong cocktail. Is Cozy's still a good place to hang out?"

"Oh, absolutely. Gigi has already added her signature holiday drinks to the menu, too."

"Okay, cool. I'd love to sit down and discuss our next moves over one of her famous cranberry bourbon blizzards. I'll head that way now."

Elle weaved between the cars blocking the intersection, then made a sharp left turn onto Oak Lane.

The trees lining the dim, narrow road created an ominous arc that loomed overhead. She slid closer to the steering wheel and pressed down on the accelerator.

"I should be at Cozy's in about ten minutes. I'm looking forward to…"

Elle's voice trailed off as a loud engine roared in the distance behind her.

Her eyes darted toward the rearview mirror. The black pickup truck that had been trailing her through the park was back.

"Oh no," she muttered.

"What's wrong?"

"I think I'm being followed."

"What?" Todd asked. "By who?"

"The same truck that was riding my bumper through the park."

Elle heard his phone shuffle, then a door slam.

"Listen," he said, "I'm jumping in my car and heading that way now. Just stay calm and be careful."

"I will." Elle turned on her bright lights and sped up. "Just get here as fast as you can. I'm heading north on Oak Lane."

"Got it. I'll stay on the line with you."

She glanced in the side-view mirror. The truck wasn't letting up. The faster she drove, the closer it got.

Elle slammed on the brakes and made a sharp right turn. Just as her car rounded the curve, the pickup rammed against the back of her car.

She screamed, jerking the steering wheel from right to left as she struggled to stay on the narrow road.

"Elle! What's going on?"

"The truck just hit me!"

Boom!

"It just hit me again!"

Elle pressed down on the accelerator. Her boot's heel tore into the floor mat.

"Hang in there," Todd said smoothly, his calm voice helping to ease her anxiety. "I'm driving as fast as I can. All this damn holiday traffic is slowing me down."

Bang!

The truck pounded into Elle's bumper again. Her car skidded off the road and careened toward a cluster of red maple trees.

Her chest hit the steering wheel. She gasped for air. Her hands ached as she clung to the wheel, struggling to guide the car away from the trees.

Elle tried to call out for Todd. But fear took hold of her vocal cords. A thin wheeze replaced the words she fought to speak.

"Stay with me, Elle. Tell me what's going on. Are you okay?"

Her body jolted uncontrollably as the vehicle bounced over the forest's uneven floor. Branches scraped against the doors. Bright red and orange leaves slammed against the windshield.

Elle leaned forward, straining to see what was up ahead. "I've been run off the road!" she finally managed to say.

The truck rammed into her once again. The car flew farther into the cluster of trees at full speed. It slid across a pile of mud then crashed into a thick gray tree trunk.

Her body thrust forward. The seat belt kept her from flying through the windshield. But the airbags failed to deploy. Her forehead slammed against the steering wheel.

Elle whimpered softly as blood trickled down her nose.

"Elle! Elle? Talk to me! What is going on?"

"I... I've been hit. Crashed into a tree."

She opened her eyes, watching as the truck sped off, then passed out.

Chapter Two

Todd glanced over at Elle, careful not to turn his head while checking on her yet again. Aside from the slight limp in her right leg and small wound on her forehead, she seemed fine.

They'd just arrived at the coroner's office to review Taylor's autopsy report. Todd was surprised when she'd insisted on going with him, considering she'd been pretty banged up the night before.

He had gotten to the forest preserve just as she was regaining consciousness. Then he'd rushed her to the hospital, relieved to hear that she didn't have a concussion. The doctors had wanted to keep her overnight for observation, but Elle had refused, saying she had work to do.

"I can see you staring at me," she said as they walked through the coroner's office parking lot.

"No, I wasn't," he lied.

But Todd's stoic demeanor broke when he opened the door to the sterile gray cement building. "Actually, you're right. I was staring at you. Because I'm concerned. Are you sure you're okay?"

"For the third time, yes. I'm good." Elle poked him playfully in the chest. "So why don't you divert those beady little eyes of yours elsewhere. They're starting to creep me out."

Todd chuckled softly, glad to hear her crack a joke. The toughness she'd exuded throughout their childhood was still there.

Despite being a scrawny kid, she had never been afraid to roll around in the dirt while playing flag football with the boys or kill spiders that crept through his sister's bedroom window.

But Elle's wiry limbs, buck teeth, corny jokes and giggly snorts were a thing of the past. She had blossomed into a stunning, poised, intelligent woman, the kind he knew only came around once in a lifetime.

Todd walked alongside Elle through the building's bland white lobby, waving at the receptionist as they approached the front desk.

"Hey, Margaret. We're here to—"

"Good afternoon," Elle interjected firmly into the Plexiglas window. "We're here to meet with Dr. Wu."

Todd watched as she began filling out the sign-in sheet. Elle was working overtime to prove that she'd recovered from the attack. He took a step back and let her.

"Hello, Deputy Jacobson," the receptionist said. She tucked her brunette bangs behind her ear and studied the visitor log. "*Aaand...* Ms. Scott. I will inform Dr. Wu that you're here. Please have a seat. I'll let you know when he's available."

Todd followed Elle over to a row of black plastic chairs. He shoved his hands inside his pockets, struggling to focus on the foggy picture windows overlooking the parking lot as they walked. But his gaze kept drifting back to her silhouette.

Elle's suede camel blazer and fitted black slacks hugged her gym-honed curves. Her slender calf muscles flexed when she strutted across the floor. She turned slightly, her pouty lips parting as she prepared to speak.

Todd forced himself to look away before taking a seat next to her.

"Did you remember to bring Taylor's file?" she asked.

"I did." He pulled it from his worn brown leather messenger bag. "I made two copies. One for me and one for you. I left the original down at the station."

"Smart. Thank you."

Elle slid the file out of his hand. Her finger grazed his thumb while her thigh brushed up against his.

A tingling rush shot up Todd's right side. He shifted in his seat and slid over, leaving a sizable gap between them.

"You all right?" she asked.

Todd kept his eyes on the file. "Yep. I'm good. So… um… I'm really curious to hear what this new coroner has to say about Taylor's autopsy report."

"Yeah, so am I. Especially considering he isn't in thrall to the sheriff's department like Dr. Winston was. I am so glad that man retired. The sheriff's office would say, 'Jump,' and he'd ask, 'How high?' Now maybe we'll get an unbiased analysis."

"I hope so. Because there's no way in hell all those scratches on Taylor's hands, forearms and legs were caused by rocks after she fell to the ground."

Elle flipped to an autopsy photo, studying it closely. "Neither was her broken neck." She handed Todd the picture. "Look, she's got red spots around her eyes, a swollen lip, blue fingernails and faint bruising around her throat. Those are all signs of strangulation. *Not* a fall on a running trail."

Todd turned the other way. "I'm sorry, Elle, but I can't look at that again. I've seen enough of my sister's dead body."

"I am so sorry," she whispered, quickly shoving the photo back inside the file.

"No need to apologize. I know you're just trying to help."

Heavy heels clicked across the dull white tile as the receptionist shuffled toward them.

"Ms. Scott, Deputy Jacobson, Dr. Wu is ready to see you now. Please, follow me."

Todd stood and took a deep breath. Elle patted his arm reassuringly.

"You've got this," she told him. "We are going to get justice for our girl. I promise."

That was all Todd needed to hear. He squared his shoulders and followed Margaret toward the coroner's office.

DR. WU PUSHED a piece of paper across his desk. Todd prayed it wasn't one of Taylor's autopsy photos. He peeked down. Let out a sigh. It was a diagram of a woman's body that had been marked up by the medical examiner.

"So, as you can both see here," Dr. Wu said, "my interpretation of Taylor's cause of death is somewhat different from Dr. Winston's. I've circled the lacerations that could, in my opinion, be defensive wounds. She's got a torn meniscus in her right knee, which is an injury that we usually see in athletes."

"Ow," Todd uttered, grabbing his leg. "I tore my meniscus back in college during a football game after being tackled to the ground by one of the opposing team's linemen. That is an excruciating injury."

"Wait," Elle interjected, "it took you being tackled by someone to sustain this injury?"

"Yes. It did."

She turned to the coroner. "So what does that tell you about Taylor's death, Dr. Wu?"

"Hold on. Before you jump to any conclusions, please note that a torn meniscus can also be caused by a hard fall. So can the broken ankle that Taylor suffered."

"But her ankle injury was pretty severe," Todd said. "She fractured both her tibia and fibula."

Dr. Wu pushed his frameless bifocals up his pockmarked nose without responding.

"Okay, then." Elle pulled a photo from Taylor's police file and placed it in front of the coroner, pointing at her white sock. "You see this?"

"I do."

"There's a muddy footprint on that sock. The pattern is consistent with the type of rubber sole that can be found on hiking boots. Look at the soles on Taylor's sneakers. That tight, grooved pattern looks nothing like the round lug pattern on the sock."

"Nice catch," Todd told her. "I didn't even notice that. So this means someone else was out on that trail with Taylor, wearing a different type of shoe. Possibly an attacker who stomped down on her ankle and broke it."

Dr. Wu eyed the photo. "Or it could've been a member of law enforcement who accidentally stepped on

Taylor's ankle and left the print during the investigation. *After* she fractured her ankle during a fall."

Todd threw his head back and stared up at the white drop ceiling.

"What about any physical evidence that could indicate foul play?" Elle asked. "Were there any skin cells found underneath Taylor's fingernails? Was there blood present? Hair follicles? Anything?"

"No," Dr. Wu replied. "There wasn't. But listen, don't get discouraged. I'm not trying to play devil's advocate here. I just want you two to view this situation from all angles. These points that I'm bringing up are the same rebuttals that the sheriff's department will present if we approach them about reopening this case."

Elle slumped forward and thumbed through the photos. Todd noticed the corners of her eyes dampen. She bit down on her bottom lip as if she wanted to say something, but didn't quite know what. The sight of her defeat unraveled him.

"You mean *when* we approach the sheriff's department," Todd told Dr. Wu.

The coroner ran his hands down the sides of his chubby face, focusing on the diagram rather than Todd's piercing stare.

"My biggest concern with Taylor's injuries is her broken hyoid bone," Dr. Wu said while drawing a circle around the figure's neck. "That type of fracture is rare."

"Except in cases of strangulation," Elle added.

"That is correct."

"That's pretty damning, don't you think? I really believe we've got enough evidence here to take to Sheriff Glover and ask that he reopen this investigation."

"I agree," Todd said, his voice cracking with frustration. "What do you think, Dr. Wu? Can we make the meeting with the sheriff's office happen?"

"Look, Sheriff Glover has full confidence in Dr. Winston's findings. So does the rest of the department. Deputy Jacobson, you work with the officers who investigated this case. I don't think they'd take too kindly to either of us butting in and demanding a reevaluation."

"At this point, I'm not concerned with my fellow officers' feelings. My top priority is finding out what happened to my sister. By any means necessary."

"Please, Dr. Wu," Elle said. "We need you. I know this case is personal for Todd and me. But emotions aside, we truly believe that law enforcement got it wrong. You seem to be on the same page as us. Your expert opinion could turn this entire case around."

The coroner looked from Elle to Todd, then down at his folded hands.

"Okay," he finally agreed. "Let's give it a try. I'll request a meeting with Sheriff Glover, present what we discussed today and see where it gets us."

"Yes!" Todd pumped his fist in the air. He stood and extended his hand. "Thank you so much, Dr. Wu. Elle and I really appreciate this."

"You're both welcome. Again, I am sorry for your loss. I just hope that in the end, you find peace."

"We'll find peace when we get justice," Todd said. "Thanks again for your time."

The moment Dr. Wu's door closed behind them, Elle threw her arms around Todd. He leaned into her embrace. Her warm hands pressed against his shoulder blades, releasing the tension in his entire upper body.

"We did it!" she exclaimed. "We are one step closer to the truth."

"Let's hope so. I'm just glad that you're here, doing this with me. I don't think I could've done it alone."

Elle slowly pulled away from him. "Well, I know I wouldn't have been able to do it without you. So, thank you for bringing me on board, partner."

Todd instinctively reached for her hand before quickly pulling back.

What in the hell are you doing?

"Hey," she continued, "we never did get that holiday drink from Cozy's, thanks to the deranged driver who crashed into me. Why don't we stop by there and grab some lunch and a couple of merry cranberry sangrias?"

"Mmm, that sounds good."

Elle pulled up Cozy's menu on her phone as they walked through the lobby. "Uh-oh. I know I shouldn't do this, but Gigi's grilled cheese and maple bacon sandwich with a side of cinnamon sweet potato fries has my name written all over it. Don't try and talk me out of ordering it, either."

"Why would I do that when I'll probably be ordering the same thing?"

Todd tucked Taylor's file inside his messenger bag. Their mission for the day was complete. Now it was time to take a respite, reconnect and focus on their next move.

Chapter Three

Elle sipped her sangria and glanced around Cozy's Café.

The quaint eatery was brimming with customers who'd taken a break from their holiday shopping to grab a bite. Every rustic wooden table was surrounded by bags and piled high with Gigi's signature sandwiches, seasonal drinks and holiday desserts.

The bright red walls were covered with twinkling string lights, evergreen garland and scented acorn wreaths. Servers bustled about in their Santa hats and reindeer headbands. Gigi, who was dressed in a Mrs. Claus apron, bounced around from table to table making sure her customers were content. Despite her petite stature, her silvery voice boomed over the festive music piping through the speakers.

"So," Todd said, "why is it that I haven't seen you around Bradford during the holidays in, like, years?"

"Ah, it's a long story."

"Well, make it short. Or not. I've got time."

Elle tilted her head, wondering just how much she should reveal. "Well, I was dating a guy named Jayson who lives in New York. He's a hedge fund manager, and—"

"Wait, Jayson Wright?"

"Yes. Do you know him?"

Todd's eyes shifted. He took a big gulp of sangria. "No. I don't. I uh… I may have seen him posted on your social media."

"Hmm, so you've been stalking my Instagram, huh?"

"Oh, no. Of course not," he replied through a toothy grin.

Elle smiled. "No worries. I kinda like the fact that you've been checking up on me."

She paused, waiting on him to make eye contact.

Todd's gaze slowly rose from his empty plate back up to her. Elle's heart flipped at the sight of his deep dimples. She pressed her hand against her chest and cleared her throat.

"So, anyway, between Jayson's schedule and mine, it was hard to find free time to take vacations. The Christmas season was our only option. I'd travel with him during the holidays, which is why you never saw me here in Bradford."

"But you're here this year."

"Yes. I am. I—I…we…um…" she stammered before choking up.

Todd reached across the table and grabbed her hand. "Hey, listen. You don't have to talk about it if you don't want to."

"No, it's fine. Jayson and I were together for three years. People are going to ask questions. I can't dodge the conversation forever."

"Hello, you two!" Gigi said as she approached the table with outstretched arms. "Elle, it's so good to see you. *Especially* during Christmastime. How have you been?"

Elle stood and embraced her. "Hello, Gigi. It's good to see you, too. I'm doing well."

"How's the food? As good as it's always been, I hope."

"Better," Elle replied. "And the signature cocktails? Incredible."

"Aw, thank you, dear. I'll clear off your table and send over another round. What are you two having for dessert?"

Todd picked up the menu. "We hadn't decided yet. These peppermint brownies look delicious. But so do the red velvet cupcakes."

"I was thinking about a slice of caramel apple cheesecake with the gingerbread crust."

"I'll tell you what," Gigi said. "Why don't I send over a platter with a little bit of all three? How does that sound?"

"That sounds like Todd is gonna have to roll me out of here on a dolly. But hey, it's the holiday season. Calories don't add up the same during this time of the year. Right?"

Gigi gave Elle a wink. "That's right, sweetie. I'll have those desserts and cocktails brought over in a moment."

Todd turned his attention back to Elle the minute Gigi left the table. "So, back to our convo. You were telling me about what happened between you and what's-his-name."

"Jayson," Elle reminded him despite knowing he hadn't forgotten. "He and I didn't see eye to eye on our future together. He was content just dating me while working nonstop, schmoozing with clients, traveling the world and obsessing over his portfolio. I wanted to settle down. Get married. Start a family. You know, like what we grew up around."

"Yeah, our parents and their friends really seem to have it all figured out."

"They do. That type of loyalty and commitment are hard to come by these days."

"Indeed," Todd agreed. "Nevertheless, I'm sorry that things didn't work out between you and Jeffrey."

"Jayson," Elle reiterated, giving Todd's arm a light pinch.

"I know, I know. Just messing with you. It's actually nice having you back in Bradford for the holidays."

"Thanks. It's nice to be back. But anyway, enough about me. How are you doing? Are you enjoying working for the sheriff's department?"

"It's cool. Just between us, this deputy sheriff training program is kicking my butt."

"How could our little hometown's sheriff's department be kicking a former marine's butt?"

"You'd be surprised. I feel like I'm back in college, pledging a fraternity. These guys are pretty much hazing me. I'm starting to think it's personal."

"I'm not surprised they're giving you a hard time. You're Bradford's hometown hero. All-star high school and college quarterback, medaled marine, boyfriend of the prettiest woman in town—"

*"Ex-*boyfriend," Todd interrupted just as a server came over with their cocktails and desserts.

"Oh," Elle uttered, pausing until the server left. "You and Jasmine broke up?"

"Yep. We did."

"I'm sorry to hear that. When did it happen?"

"Earlier this year. The day after Valentine's Day, to be exact. I gave her a gold necklace, which she didn't like, considering she was expecting an engagement ring."

"You two had discussed marriage?"

"She'd brought up the subject on occasion. But I pretty much avoided the topic."

Elle's gaze fell. "Hmm, so you're not interested in getting married…"

"No, it's not that. I wasn't interested in marrying Jasmine. But I'm looking forward to marriage and starting a family. It just has to be with the right person."

Elle slowly raised her head. She and Todd locked eyes just as Gigi approached the table.

"How's everything tasting?" she asked.

"We've been so busy chatting that we haven't had a chance to dig in yet," Elle said.

"Well, hurry up and try everything out! I added a few new ingredients to this year's recipes, and I'm anxious to hear what you two think. Oh! And before you leave, stop by the coffee counter. I'm experimenting with a new gingerbread espresso and would love to hear your thoughts on it."

"Mmm, that sounds good," Todd said. "We'll see you on the way out."

The moment Gigi left the table, someone else approached.

"Elle? Elle Scott? Is that you?"

She spun around.

"Rachel! Hey!" Elle said to her former high school classmate. "How are you?"

"I'm doing well. Just shocked to see you in here in Bradford. No exotic overseas vacation this Christmas?"

"Long story, but no. We'll have to discuss all that another time. Preferably over cocktails."

"Sounds like a plan." The curvy, green-eyed redhead flipped her hair over her shoulder before giving Todd a sympathetic wave. "Hey, how are you holding up, my friend?"

"I'm hanging in there. It's been tough, dealing with Taylor's death and all. But my family and I are doing the best we can to get through it. Having Elle here to support us has been a tremendous help."

"I'm sure it has." Rachel paused. "Elle, are you still working as a private investigator?"

Elle pressed her finger against her lips. "I am. But please, keep that information confidential. Most people in Bradford don't know about my practice. I'd like to keep it that way."

"Gotcha. Well, I have some information that I'd like to share with you two. Confidentially. My sister, Faith, still works at the bank, and she ran by me some interesting transactions that were made by Taylor shortly before her death. And I'm assuming you've already looked into that women's organization Taylor was heavily involved with. The Precious Jewels."

"The precious what?" Todd asked before grabbing his phone and pulling up the Notes app.

"The Precious Jewels. It's a social club of sorts, run by some of the wealthiest, most obnoxious women in town."

"Really?" Elle said. "That doesn't sound like the type of crowd Taylor would normally associate with. I mean, she did always aspire to attain the finer things in life. She just never had the money to do so."

Rachel glanced around the café, then bent down.

"Yeah, well, this little club was beginning to change all that for her," she whispered. "It was actually a front for a major pyramid scheme."

A sick feeling churned inside Elle's stomach.

Taylor was keeping secrets from me...

"I didn't know anything about this," Elle said while opening the calendar on her phone. "But we'd definitely like to hear more. When are you available to meet?"

Rachel reached inside her handbag and pulled out a business card. "I'll make myself available whenever you are. The sooner the better. Because unlike the sheriff's department, I don't believe that Taylor's death was an accident."

"Yeah, neither do we," Todd said. "We'll give you a call tomorrow and set something up. Thanks for passing along whatever information you have. We really appreciate it."

"Of course. I'm happy to help in whatever way I can. Talk to you soon."

Todd pushed the platter of desserts toward Elle. "I just lost my appetite. But feel free to dive in."

"At this point, I'll pass as well. This day has been a lot. *Too* much."

"Why don't we get this wrapped up and take it to go? I'll drop you off at home, and we can reconvene tomorrow."

"That works for me."

Elle stood and threw on her red wool trench coat, her mind now racing in a thousand different directions. From the pyramid scheme to whatever other secrets Taylor had been harboring, Elle felt as though she no longer knew her best friend.

Oh, Taylor, what had you gotten yourself into?

Chapter Four

Elle pulled into the parking lot of the Bradford Museum of Contemporary Art and glanced down at her watch. She was running a few minutes late for her meeting with Rachel, who served as the museum's curator.

Her father's old sky blue Toyota Camry backfired loudly the minute she turned off the engine.

Elle ducked down, startled by what sounded like a piercing gunshot. She peered over the steering wheel. Two little boys burst out crying while clinging to their mother's legs. A short, stout security guard hustled toward her car.

"Oh, God," Elle moaned, embarrassed by the commotion she'd caused.

"Ma'am, are you okay?" he asked.

She rolled down the window and forced a smile. "I'm fine. Just dealing with an old car that probably needs a tune-up."

The guard removed his cap and scratched his balding head. "I'd have to agree with you there. Sounds like you've got an issue with the engine belts, too. Why don't you pop the hood and let me take a look at it?"

"Thank you for offering, but I'm actually running late for a meeting," Elle said just as her cell phone rang.

The guard coughed when a cloud of black smoke drifted from the back of the car. "All right. But I'd advise you to go get your vehicle checked out as soon as possible. I'd hate for it to stop on you out here. Especially on one of these dark, desolate roads, late at night—"

"I appreciate your help," Elle interrupted. "I need to take this call."

"Suit yourself…" He lingered for a few seconds longer, staring at her intently before finally walking off.

"Weird," Elle muttered before picking up the call. "Hello?"

"Hey, it's Todd."

"Oh, hey. I didn't recognize the number you're calling from."

"I'm using one of the phones at the sheriff's office. My cell is dead."

"Wait, you're not on your way to the museum?"

"No, that's why I'm calling. We had an extra training session added to the agenda today. A law enforcement officer from Cane County who specializes in human trafficking came in to speak with us. Apparently he's one of the best in the state and hard to schedule. So we had to fit him in."

Elle grabbed the handle and bumped her body against the door three times before it finally opened. "I'm bummed that you can't make it. But I'll be sure to take good notes during the meeting. I really wish you could be here."

"Yeah, me, too. Maybe we can get together once you're done and go over everything you and Rachel discuss. I mean, if you're available," Todd quickly added.

She smiled at the nervousness in his shaky tone. It

was cute, coming from such a tough guy. "I'm available. I'll give you a call when I'm leaving."

"Cool. Talk to you soon."

Elle rushed through the parking lot and climbed the curved cement staircase leading up to the museum's carved teakwood doors.

Posted near the entrance, the security guard shuffled his tiny feet back and forth as he eyed Elle hungrily, his bloated hands hanging from his worn leather belt.

"Don't forget to get that car checked out," he said with a wink. "If you need a recommendation for a good mechanic, I've got just the guy for you."

"I'll keep that in mind. Thanks."

The guard opened the door for her. She quickly slipped inside before he could say another word.

Elle pulled out her phone to text Rachel just as she appeared from around the corner.

Everyone stopped and stared as Rachel strutted through the lobby wearing a gorgeous emerald green wrap dress and six-inch nude stilettos. She waved at Elle, oblivious to the attention.

"Hey, glad you could make it."

"Of course. Thank you for inviting me," Elle said, feeling underdressed in her black leather blazer, jeans and combat boots. "I am so sorry I'm late. My father's car was acting up, then Todd called to tell me that he wouldn't be able to make it."

"So it's just gonna be us girls?"

"Yep, just us."

"That's fine," Rachel said. "Knowing you, I'm sure you'll take meticulous notes for him. Follow me. Let's talk in my office. We'll have plenty of privacy there."

Rachel led Elle through a maze of ten-foot-tall

bronze sculptures. They walked down a long, stark white hallway where the walls were covered in bold, colorful, abstract paintings. The museum's subtle Christmas decor consisted of elegant crystal ornaments dangling from the ceilings and large evergreen wreaths hanging from the arched windows.

Elle followed Rachel into a spacious, minimalist office. Soft gray walls matched the hardwood floors. An off-white oval desk sat in the middle of the floor.

"Have a seat," Rachel said, pointing toward a pair of Eames-style yellow swivel chairs. "Can I get you anything to drink? Water, tea, coffee? Something a little stronger?"

"Thanks, but no. I'm fine. I love your space. This is really cool."

"Thank you."

Elle sensed an immediate change in Rachel's demeanor as soon as they sat down. She stared at her hands while fidgeting with her manicured, chocolate brown nails. Her lips tightened as her eyes grew weepy.

"I know this isn't easy, Rachel. That's why I'm here. Todd and I are going to do all that we can to get to the bottom of Taylor's death."

"I hope so." She fanned her face. "*Whew.* I'd better pull myself together. I've got a meeting with an artist later this afternoon and would hate to scare him off with a swollen crying face."

Elle pulled a couple of tissues out of her tote bag. "Here. Dry your eyes, take a deep breath and let's talk."

Rachel inhaled slowly. "Where should I even start?"

"How about with Taylor's husband, Bryce?" Elle asked, cracking open her notebook. "Even though the sheriff's department declared Taylor's death as accidental, I know they spoke with him. He was working at the car dealership that he manages, Capital Motors, during the time that she died. Not that he needs an alibi or anything, but in the event that he does, he's got one."

"*Allegedly.* Do you know how easy it is for him to slip in and out of that dealership without being seen? He also has access to every car on the lot. He could've driven one of the dealership's vehicles to the park rather than his own. His personal car would've remained in the work lot, making it look as if he was still there when he actually wasn't."

"That's true," Elle replied while rigorously taking notes. "I'll ask Todd whether the sheriff's department watched any of the dealership's video surveillance footage from that day. If Bryce did in fact leave work at any given point, it should've been recorded."

She didn't know if Taylor's marriage was happy or if she and her husband had been having difficulties. It was something she wanted to pursue, but carefully.

Elle took a deep breath and glanced over at the twinkling yellow string lights lining Rachel's window. They resembled the ones she and Taylor would drape along her windowsills and canopy bed during the holidays.

Stop it. Stay in the moment before you burst into tears.

"When I ran into you at Cozy's," she continued, "you mentioned some strange bank transactions that Taylor made. Can you tell me more about those?"

Rachel opened her laptop and tapped on the keyboard. "I sure can. My sister didn't email me the bank statements, because that would've been illegal. But she did send me an email summarizing the activity.

On a hypothetical account, of course," she added with a wink.

She spun the computer around. Elle zoomed in on the screen.

"Okay, so Taylor took out a second mortgage on the house. Why is that strange?"

"Because her husband didn't know about it. He came into the bank ranting about how Taylor had forged his signature on the paperwork. The manager reviewed the documents and realized that Bryce's signature didn't match those on the docs."

Elle tapped her fingers against her chin. "How did Taylor pull that off? The underwriter should've caught it before approving the loan."

"Not if the underwriter is a member of Taylor's little social club that I was telling you about. The Precious Jewels."

"Oh," Elle breathed, sitting back in her chair. "I see. Wow. I guess I'd be angry, too, if I were Bryce."

Rachel's right eyebrow arched. "Angry enough to kill? Because a few months after Bryce found out about the second mortgage, Taylor was found dead."

"Humph." Elle slammed her notebook down on the desk. "I would question why the sheriff's department didn't look into any of this. But I already know. They don't want a stain on Bradford's reputation. It's easier to declare a death as accidental than to admit that there's a killer in the community."

"Which is a scary thought," Rachel said.

"What other transactions did your sister mention in that email?"

"Taylor had been making several random deposits. The personal checks were made payable to her, and the amounts were pretty high. I'm talking in the thousands. I think they were payments coming from women who were entering into The Precious Jewels' pyramid scheme."

"Interesting…"

Rachel slid the laptop closer toward Elle. "Here's a picture of several members at Bradford's holiday charity ball last year."

Elle studied the photo. About twenty women were standing in front of the town's historic cultural center. They were dressed in floor-length ball gowns, with their hair twisted into dramatic chignons and botoxed faces covered in heavy makeup. Each of them held a glass of champagne high in the air.

Taylor was standing off to the side, holding several handbags. Her red knee-length taffeta dress didn't quite fit in with the rest of the group's couture formalwear.

"I guess Taylor wasn't a member back then, huh," Elle said.

"Not yet. But a lot had changed since then. Taylor worked her way in by schmoozing with the right people, then pulling together enough money to pay the entry fee. Once she was in, she recruited other members like nobody's business and rose to the top pretty quickly. But I heard that there was a lot of dissension within the group. Not everyone approved of Taylor's presence, nor her tactics. Especially the ringleader, Sloane Whitlock."

"Wait, how do you know all this?"

"The museum is used for charity events, and I've overheard things from some in that group."

Elle slowly nodded. "Okay, and who is Sloane Whitlock?"

"The infamous founder of The Precious Jewels. And one of the richest, most powerful women in Bradford."

Elle wrote the woman's name down, then sighed heavily. "Wow. I've been away for way too long. There is so much going on that I didn't know about."

"That's why I'm here. To help fill in the gaps. If you want to get to the bottom of Taylor's death, you're gonna have to refamiliarize yourself with the town. A lot's changed since you've been gone." Rachel opened her drawer and pulled out a flyer. "I'd suggest you start by attending this year's holiday charity ball. All of The Precious Jewels will be there. Including Sloane. It's where she likes to go and scope out potential new members."

Elle picked up the glossy, red-and-green invitation. "This is taking place next weekend. But it looks like I've still got time to RSVP. Are you going?"

Rachel snorted loudly. "Hell no. That's not my scene. I'd rather have my teeth pulled than spend an evening with those awful women."

"Maybe I can get Todd to go with me."

"I'm sure he'd love that. And not just for investigative purposes…"

Elle scoffed at Rachel's sly grin.

"Will you stop that? Todd and I are just friends. And partners now that we're working together on this case. That's all."

"Yeah, okay, *that's all*. I saw the way you two were acting toward one another at Cozy's. The long stares, the unnecessary touching. Looked to me like there was a lot more going on than just two people working on a case."

Elle's skin prickled underneath her blazer. She tugged at the collar and cleared her throat.

"I should probably get going. You've got a meeting coming up, and I'd like to get these notes organized before I talk to Todd. You gave me a lot of good intel. I can't thank you enough."

"It's the least I could do," Rachel said as she walked Elle out. "I'm happy to help in any way that I can. If there's anything else I can do, or anything else you need, just let me know."

"I will. And I'll keep you posted on the charity gala, too. I have a feeling that event just may open up a whole new angle to this investigation."

"I'm sure it will. Talk soon."

Chapter Five

"We haven't gotten any leads on the black pickup truck that rammed into you at the forest preserve," Todd said.

"That's disappointing to hear," Elle muttered, staring down at the dusty earth beneath her boots.

"The sheriff's department is still working on it, though. So don't lose hope."

"I'll try…"

Todd cringed at the doubt in her low tone. The mood between them was already somber as they walked along the River Birch Park's desolate trail, studying the path that Taylor used to run.

An eerie feeling lingered in the air. Tree branches seemed to move a bit slower. A cold sprinkle of rain fell from the gray afternoon sky. The howling wind was reminiscent of whining, tortured souls.

"I've lost faith in our town's sheriff's department," Elle said. "I still can't believe they didn't put more effort into Taylor's death investigation. So it's not surprising that they have no answers for me."

"My hope is that I can help turn things around now that I'm a part of the agency. It's just gonna take some time. And a lot of effort. Starting with those leads Rachel gave you yesterday."

"Yes, because coming out here time and time again hasn't produced anything new. I've been praying that we'd stumble upon some sort of overlooked evidence. Or a rock stuck in the dirt near where Taylor fell. Or even a small ditch. *Something* that would explain how she could've fallen and broken her neck on a seemingly even trail that she'd been running for years."

Elle looked to the sky as a beam of light shone through two parting clouds.

"I wish Taylor would somehow speak to us," she whispered. "Tell us what really happened to her. Guide us to the evidence so we won't have to keep returning to the place where she was murdered. It's becoming too painful."

Todd wrapped his arm around Elle. "I know it is. But just remember, you're not in this alone. I'm here with you, every step of the way. The answers are going to come."

"Isn't it a shame that so far, our best intel came from an art curator rather than the sheriff's department?"

"In all fairness, the department did talk to Bryce. They just took him at his word when he said he was at work during the time of Taylor's death. And as for that women's group Taylor was a part of, the uh…"

"The Precious Jewels."

"Right. The Precious Jewels. Sheriff Glover thinks they're just a superficial social club filled with gossipy women. I don't think he even knows about the pyramid scheme they're allegedly running."

Elle approached the tulip tree where Taylor's body

had been found. She crossed her arms over her chest and turned to Todd. "Yeah, well, that's why I've got to figure out a way to infiltrate the group. See if I can find out exactly what was going on with Taylor before her death. If she was at odds with the group's founder, and there was a lot of money at stake, then that could very well be the cause of her murder."

"Which is why we'll be front and center at that gala next weekend." Todd bent down, studying the tree's bark. "But before that, I'd like for us to stop by Taylor's house and pay Bryce a visit. Because you're right. There may be more to his involvement now that we know about that second mortgage."

"Do you think you could get ahold of his car dealership's surveillance footage from the day Taylor died?"

"Possibly. I'll look into the list of employees and see if I know anyone who works there. I would try and go through the sheriff's department. But at this point that wouldn't be a good look considering the case is technically closed. I'm sure it'll remain that way until we can present enough evidence to Sheriff Glover convincing him to reopen it."

Elle reached inside the pocket of her black yoga jacket and pulled out her cell phone. "Do you see anything down there?"

"Nope. Nothing."

"I'm gonna call Bryce and see if he's home. If he is, I'll tell him I want to stop by and give him my condolences in person."

"Good idea. Because this crime scene isn't giving us anything."

"Except a morbid feeling of dread," Elle replied as she dialed Bryce's number.

THE FIRST THING Todd noticed when Bryce opened the door was his puffy red eyes. He looked to have dropped a good ten pounds from his five-foot-ten-inch frame.

Todd opened his mouth to speak, but nothing came out. The shock of Bryce's appearance took hold of his brain.

"Bryce, I am so sorry for your loss," Elle said, giving him a warm embrace.

"Thank you," he croaked. "It—it's been tough."

"I can imagine."

Bryce sniffled into a tissue and stepped aside, letting them enter.

The living room was in complete disarray. Half-empty take-out containers and dirty dishes were strewn about. A pillow and blankets covered the taupe suede couch. The Christmas decorations Taylor normally hung up right after Thanksgiving were still in boxes, scattered around the room.

"Sorry, guys," Bryce said, quickly clearing the sofa. "As you can see, I have been living out of this room. I've barely stepped foot in the bedroom since Taylor…"

His words transitioned into a long sob. Todd reached over and grabbed his shoulder.

"I am so sorry, man."

"Thanks. I just—I miss my wife. How are you and the family doing? I tried calling your mom this morning, but she didn't pick up."

"Yeah, she's having a tough time. Don't take it personally. My father and I are the only two people she's been able to talk to."

"Understandable. Please, have a seat. I did manage to make a batch of that sweet Christmas tea Taylor loved, with the apple cider and cranberry juice mix. It was our holiday tradition. Even though this year, I've been adding quite a bit of vodka to mine. But anyway, would either of you like a glass?"

"I'd love some," Elle said. "Thanks."

Todd slowly sat down. "I would, too. I'm pretty thirsty. Elle and I just came from the park's hiking trail where Taylor's body was found."

Bryce froze, staring straight ahead as if digesting what Todd just told him. Several moments of silence passed before he shuffled over to the dining room table and poured their tea.

Todd watched his hands closely for signs of nervous trembling. There were none.

"Did you all find anything out there?" Bryce finally asked.

"No, unfortunately. But we're gonna keep looking until we do."

Bryce handed them their glasses, then paced the floor a few times before sitting on the edge of the love seat. "I've actually gone to the scene to see what I could find. I came up empty, too. Then when I went into the station to speak with Sheriff Glover, he told me that his guys combed the area thoroughly. They didn't come up with any evidence proving Taylor's death wasn't accidental."

"So you're okay talking about Taylor's passing?" Elle asked. "Because if not, we won't—"

"No, no," Bryce interrupted. "I'm fine talking about it. I actually *want* to talk about it. Especially with you two. I'd love to get your take on the whole thing."

"Good," Todd said. "You and I haven't really had a chance to discuss any of this. And I honestly feel more comfortable having this conversation outside of the sheriff's department."

"So do I. Because, trust me, it hasn't gone over my head that some folks in Bradford think I had something to do with this. The scrutiny only gets magnified when I'm sitting in the station being questioned by authorities."

Todd propped his elbows onto his knees. "Well, we're not here to interrogate you. We go too far back for all that. We just wanna hear what you think, and try to figure out what really happened to the woman we all loved dearly."

"Absolutely," Bryce choked, pressing his knuckles against the corners of his eyes.

"I know this is hard for you," Elle said softly, "but do you really believe that Taylor stumbled and fell on the trail? Or do you think there's more to her death?"

"At this point, I don't know what to believe. Taylor ran that path almost every day for years. She knew it so well. For her to fall and break her neck on it doesn't make sense to me. Is it possible? Yes. But is it likely? I don't believe so."

Todd observed him closely, looking for any signs of suspicion.

Bryce had broken eye contact the minute Elle asked what he thought really happened to Taylor. He licked his lips several times while rubbing his right palm against his knee. He stared down at the floor, pausing in between sentences as if searching for responses within the fibers of the beige carpeting.

Todd glanced over at Elle. She stared back at him,

her eyelids lowered. He had a feeling they were thinking the same thing. Bryce's body language seemed suspicious even if he was agreeing that Taylor's death didn't look accidental.

"So you believe there's a possibility that Taylor's death wasn't accidental?" Todd asked.

"Yes. I do think that's a possibility."

"But who would want to kill Taylor? And why?"

Bryce's breathing quickened. He swiped his hand across his creased forehead, which suddenly appeared damp.

"Look," he began, "I don't wanna wrongly pin my wife's death on anyone. But I will say this. Taylor had been hanging out with this group of women who were involved in some type of money grabbing scheme. I don't know much about it, because Taylor kept a lot of what was going on hidden from me. What I do know is that some of the women were making a lot of money. And in order to make money, you have to spend money, which is where my problem with Taylor came into play."

Todd paused, almost spilling his tea as he raised his glass to his lips.

"Taylor was doing a lot of spending?" Elle asked.

"Yes. To the point where she took out a second mortgage on our house behind my back."

Bryce's cell phone rang. He grabbed it off the coffee table. "I need to take this. Could you please excuse me?"

"Of course."

Todd turned to Elle as soon as Bryce sauntered into the kitchen. "I'm surprised he told us about the second mortgage," he whispered.

"*And* that he had a problem with Taylor's spending. I guess he doesn't think we'd ever suspect him of hurting her."

"It's so convenient that he's pointing the finger at The Precious Jewels. Plus he's supposedly got an alibi. I really need to try and get ahold of his dealership's surveillance footage."

"Yeah, you do," Elle agreed. "Because if Bryce's sweating, heavy breathing and lip licking are any indication of guilt, that man is far from innocent."

Todd glanced down at a pile of bills that were hanging off the glass end table. The word *OVERDUE* had been stamped in red across several of them.

He took a closer look. Charges ranging in the hundreds, a few in the thousands, were highlighted in yellow.

Todd quickly straightened up when Bryce walked back into the living room.

He appeared to have more pep in his step. A bit of a bounce even. The creases in his forehead were gone, as was the sheet of perspiration covering his deep brown skin.

"Sorry for the interruption," Bryce said. "That was my agent calling about Taylor's life insurance policy."

Todd and Elle sat silently, waiting for him to elaborate. He didn't. Instead, he poured himself a glass of tea and took a long sip.

"So," Bryce continued, "like I was saying, Taylor had gotten involved with this secretive women's group that had some sort of strange money scheme going on. She wouldn't tell me anything about it. But when I started seeing all these charges on my credit card bills for extravagant new clothes and shoes, and large charitable donations being made, I knew something was up."

"Hmm, that's interesting," Elle said. "You know, Taylor told me about several of the get-rich schemes she'd invested in over the years. All the work-from-home opportunities, multilevel marketing services, promises to help her open a business. The list was never-ending. But she always had to put money up before she made anything back. Most times, she never turned a profit."

Bryce snorted. "Yeah, tell me about it. My salary was financing all those schemes. Including this last one she was involved in before she died."

Todd noticed a glint in Elle's eyes. He knew she was egging Bryce on in hopes that he'd start spilling more than he intended.

In that moment, he was overcome by a strong mix of admiration and attraction. Seeing Elle in action had him smitten.

"So, Todd," Bryce said. "Has the sheriff's department looked into The Positive Gems yet?"

Todd hesitated.

Don't reveal too much...

"The Precious Jewels," he corrected. "And um…yes. The sheriff's department has looked into the group. As far as I know, nothing suspicious came up."

"Humph." Bryce slammed his glass down onto the coffee table, then stood. "Well, I appreciate you both coming by to check on me. But I need to get going. I was supposed to be at the dealership thirty minutes ago."

They followed him to the door. Elle placed her hand on his arm.

"Thanks for letting us stop by on such short notice. Hang in there. Todd and I are doing everything in our power to get justice for Taylor."

Bryce's body stiffened up. Elle quickly snatched her hand away.

"That—that's good," he stammered. "Keep me posted on whatever you find out."

Both Todd and Elle ignored the request.

"If you think of anything that could help with our investigation," Todd said, "give me a call. No lead is too small."

Bryce nodded as his chin began to quiver. "I will. Oh…wait!" He ran toward one of the end tables and shuffled through the pile of bills.

"What is he doing?" Elle muttered.

"I have no idea."

Bryce pulled out a notebook and handed it to Todd. "What is this?" he asked.

"A book that Taylor used to track the new members she recruited into The Positive Gems."

Todd opened his mouth to correct him again.

Don't even bother. Just let him finish.

"She kept up with all the names, initiation fees that were paid and what I'm assuming are levels that members reached over time. It's weird. They referred to themselves as different gemstones. Rubies and Emeralds and whatnot. I don't know. I couldn't make sense of it all. But I figured it might offer up some new leads. So I'm handing it off to you two."

"Good looking out," Todd said. "We'll definitely check it out."

"If I think of anything else that might help with the investigation, I'll give you a call."

Todd and Elle said their goodbyes. They didn't speak a word to each other on the way to the car.

As soon as the doors were closed, he turned to her.

"I'm still not convinced that Bryce is innocent in all this."

"Neither am I. He seems to be harboring a lot of anger over the way Taylor mishandled their finances."

"You should've seen the pile of overdue credit card bills sitting next to the couch. Maybe that's why his mood suddenly lifted after he got that call about Taylor's life insurance policy. I wonder if he's expecting a big payout."

"Could be." Elle closed her eyes and pressed her hand against her forehead. "As far as I'm concerned, Bryce is still a suspect."

"Absolutely. But aside from that, I'm looking forward to attending the charity gala and finding out what The Precious Jewels are all about."

Chapter Six

Elle stood in front of the mirror hanging from the back of her bedroom door. Her hair was slicked back into a flawless bun. Her shimmery nude makeup had been expertly applied by a Lancôme specialist at the mall. The strapless midnight blue dress she'd borrowed from her cousin fit as if it had been designed just for her.

Everything appeared perfect. Except that it wasn't.

"Get your head on straight," Elle told herself.

She sat down on the bed and slipped her feet inside a pair of sparkly silver pumps. Taylor's notebook was lying next to her. It was still open to the page that read more like a journal entry than a recruitment registry.

It was dated five days before her death.

Elle was certain that Bryce had overlooked it. Had he not, maybe he would've thought twice before passing the book on.

She grabbed it and reread the haunting admission for a third time.

I'm afraid. Too afraid to share this with anyone. So I'm pouring it all out right here on these pages. Maybe writing it down will put an end to the harassment. Somehow...

Someone is after me. Messaging me. Emailing me. Following me. Trying to scare me. I know it's one of my recruits. Maybe Sloane was right. Maybe I did open my circle up too wide. Let too many people in. People who weren't right for The Precious Jewels organization.

My recruits are angry with me and I feel terrible about it. But what can I do? They knew what they were getting themselves into. It isn't my fault they haven't been able to enlist new members, move up in the ranks and earn the treasure chest. I've worked my ass off to get to where I am. I earned that treasure, and I shouldn't feel guilty now that it's my turn to collect it. And not half of it this go round. ALL of it. My recruits should be inspired, not bitter.

But someone is angry. Angry enough to threaten my life. They don't want to see me win. They'd rather see me dead.

I can't go to the police. They'll dig too deep and find a way to disband our organization. I refuse to ruin this opportunity, for myself or my fellow sisters.

I'm finally where I want to be in life. It's my time. I deserve this. I will get rich or die trying. Scared or not, I refuse to let empty threats stop me.

I am going to press on toward the goal. Collect the treasure chest. Then move on to bigger and better things...

A teardrop fell onto the page, smudging the black ink. Elle didn't realize she'd been crying.

Stop it. Put the book away. Focus on tonight and the mission at hand.

But Elle was having a hard time following her own advice. Taylor's message was so unsettling. Especially the ending.

What bigger and better things were you moving on to?

Elle's phone buzzed just as she picked up her clutch. Her heart thumped. She checked the caller ID. It was Todd.

She sighed with relief.

"Hey," Elle rasped. "What's up?"

"I'm heading your way now. Are you ready to hit this gala and do your thing?"

Elle's eyes fell to the floor. She cleared her throat. "Yep. I'm ready."

Todd went silent for a moment.

"Wait, what's going on?" he asked. "Are you okay?"

"Yeah!" she blurted out too eagerly. "I mean, yes. I'm good. Why?"

"Because you sound strange. Like something's bothering you."

Just tell him...

Elle stood and began pacing the floor. "I…um… I received a weird phone call today. Voice mail, actually. Someone called me anonymously and I didn't pick up. So they left a message."

"*Okay*…what did the message say?"

"That they know what I'm doing. And if I don't stop, I won't make it out of the next attack alive."

Todd grunted into the phone. "The next attack? What the hell is that supposed to mean?"

"That whoever called had something to do with the

crash at the forest preserve, and they're planning the next move against me."

Elle's legs trembled uncontrollably. She stumbled over to her vanity and slumped down onto the white wooden stool.

"Was it a man or a woman?"

"I couldn't tell."

"Well, what did the person's voice sound like?" Todd asked.

"Very eerie. And deep. But cartoonish. Like they were speaking into one of those devices that disguise your voice." Elle grabbed a tissue and dabbed it along her forehead. "Isn't it ironic that I got that call right after we went to visit Bryce?"

"It is. Or it could just be a coincidence. Either way, we'll get to the bottom of it. But in the meantime, you need to be careful. Somebody's obviously watching you. Keep your eyes open. Be mindful of how you move around town. Of course I'll be looking out for you, as well."

"Thanks, Todd. I'm just… I'm nervous."

"That's understandable. But trust me, you and I will get to whoever is behind this before they get to you. You're a highly skilled private investigator. I'm a former marine turned deputy sheriff. Together, we're a force to be reckoned with."

A surge of confidence shot through Elle's chest. She stood, grabbed her clutch and headed to the living room. "I need that reminder, Todd. Sometimes I forget to stand in my power."

"Never forget that, my friend. Listen, I'm pulling up to your house now. Are you ready?"

"I am. Let's do this."

Todd wrapped his arm around Elle's waist and led her up the Bradford Cultural Center's winding marble staircase. She held on to the railing, careful not to disrupt the decorative cedar garland.

All eyes were on the pair when they reached the landing. Elle glanced around the vast lobby, taking in the elegant Christmas decor. Snowy wreaths hung from the walls, and large red poinsettias stood at each ballroom entryway.

A twelve-foot-tall Douglas fir stood in the corner. Its twinkling lights and crystal ornaments shone brightly as guests took photos in front of the majestic tree.

Elle was surprised when Todd's hand remained on the small of her back. His touch caused a tingling sensation to dance across her skin. She forced herself to ignore it and focus on the smiling faces greeting them while they walked through the atrium.

This is not a date. Stay focused on why you're here...

But that wouldn't be easy. Elle had almost forgotten the reason they were attending the gala the moment Todd showed up at her house.

His freshly trimmed hair and goatee framed his handsome face perfectly. His slim-fitting tuxedo accentuated his muscular physique. The sexy scent of bergamot lingered on his neck. The sensual way in which he'd clutched her hand while helping her to the car was reminiscent of a date night versus an investigative mission.

It didn't help matters when Todd kept telling her how beautiful she looked.

"*Hello*, Earth to Elle."

She snapped back into the moment as Todd led her inside the grand ballroom.

"Did you hear me?" he asked.

"No, I'm sorry. What'd you say?"

"I asked if you'd like a glass of champagne." He stopped and turned to her. "Are you sure you're okay?"

"I'm fine." She gazed out at the crowd, watching as partygoers laughed, danced and drank with one another. "I was just thinking about how nice it would be if we were here under different circumstances. More pleasant circumstances. With Taylor by our side."

Todd inhaled sharply. "I know. But she's here with us in spirit. Seems like I can feel her presence everywhere I go."

"Same here. I'm just hoping her spirit will lead us in the right direction with this investigation."

"Knowing Taylor, I'm sure it will."

A server walked by carrying a tray filled with glasses of champagne.

"Would either of you like a cocktail?" she asked.

"I'd love one," Elle said. "Thank you."

She and Todd took two flutes, then slowly circled the room.

"Why don't we go and check out the items that are up for auction?" he asked.

"Good idea. I think some of the women standing over by the jewelry table were in that photo of The Precious Jewels Rachel showed me." Elle ran her hands along the sides of her dress and squared her shoulders. "Time for me to go and work my magic."

"I'm right beside you."

They strolled over to the far end of the ballroom, past the oil paintings of the town's past politicians hanging on the carved wood paneling.

Elle casually approached the table and gazed at the

sparkling earrings, necklaces and bracelets. She pretended to read through the descriptions of each piece while listening in on the women's conversation.

"Did you put in a bid for the vacation in Oahu?" one of them asked.

"The one that Suzanne and her husband donated? Absolutely not. You couldn't pay me to stay in that run-down shack they like to call a picturesque plantation home."

The trio burst into a fit of cackling snorts.

"Wow, tough crowd," Todd murmured.

"They sound more like a herd of laughing hyenas than a group of sophisticated ladies. I can't believe Taylor would've wanted to be around women like that."

"You know my sister. She was a wonderful person who had a penchant for the finer things in life. Unfortunately, she was willing to go to any length to attain them."

"Ladies!" someone shrieked. "I am so sorry I'm late! The couture seamstress I hired to alter my dress made a complete mess of it. I had to pull this old rag out the back of my closet at the last minute. I am so embarrassed!"

Elle watched through the corners of her eyes as the woman ran her perfectly manicured hands, which were draped in vintage cocktail rings, over her size zero frame. Her floor-length black silk dress appeared to be brand-new. A stunning pearl and rhinestone belt cinched her tiny waist.

"So," she continued, "please, pardon my tardiness."

"Oh, come on, Sloane," one of the women said. "You know you look marvelous."

"And I'm sure you don't need any of us to tell you that," another chimed in.

Elle leaned in and whispered in Todd's ear, "Sloane Whitlock is the founder of The Precious Jewels."

"Got it."

Sloane flipped her sleek platinum blond bob over her shoulder and waved her friends off. "You all are just saying that to make me feel better. But keep going. Because it's working!"

A rotund brunette came waddling over to the group.

"Ladies!" she wheezed while tugging at her tight floral gown. "Have you seen any new prospects here tonight? The Precious Jewels are in desperate need of new members."

"I just arrived not too long ago," Sloane told her. "So I haven't had a chance to make my rounds just yet. But my eyes and ears are definitely open."

Elle grabbed an onyx choker off the table and held it to her neck. "What do you think of this piece?" she asked Todd. "It's gorgeous, isn't it? I've got some extra cash to play around with, plus the proceeds will go toward a good cause, so…"

The group of women fell silent. Elle could feel their eyes on her. She acted as if she didn't notice.

Todd reached out and touched the delicate stones. Her skin shivered beneath the warmth of his fingertips.

"I think it looks beautiful," he said. "Let's bid on it."

Sloane pushed her friends aside and slowly approached Elle.

"Excuse me, but I don't think we've met. My name is Sloane Whitlock. I'm on the board of directors here at the cultural center. And you are?"

"Elle. Elle Scott. It's nice to meet you."

"Likewise," Sloane purred, gently shaking her hand. "And your husband is right. That choker looks absolutely stunning on you."

"Thank you. But this isn't my husband. He's actually—"

"Todd Jacobson," the chubby redhead interrupted. "Taylor's brother. I remember meeting you at the funeral." She grabbed his hand. "Oh, honey, I am so sorry for your loss. How are you and your family holding up?"

"We're hanging in there. Thank you for asking."

Elle peered over at Sloane. Her gaunt cheeks reddened underneath streaks of bronzer. Her overly plumped lips parted, then tightened, then parted again, as if she wanted to say something but couldn't find the words.

What are you holding back?

"So," Elle said to her, "you think I should bid on this choker?"

Sloane pressed her hand against her bony chest. "I certainly do. It's gorgeous. *You're* gorgeous. I'd say you two are a match made in heaven."

"Aw, how sweet. Thank you."

"I don't believe I've ever seen you here at our charity event. Is this your first time?"

"Yes, it is. I grew up in Bradford but moved to New York years ago. I rarely get back to town for the holidays. But this year was different. I'm so glad I was able to come home and spend it with my family."

"Ah, very nice. New York is one of my favorite cities in the world. What is it that you do there?"

"I…um—I'm a consultant," Elle lied. "An image consultant."

"And how long will you be in town?"

"I'm not sure. Right now, indefinitely. I haven't seen my family in quite some time, so I'd like to stick around for a while."

Elle could feel Sloane scrutinizing her. Making sure she was someone worthy of an invitation into her fold.

Keep doing what you're doing. It's working.

"I'm also looking forward to reconnecting with old friends," she continued. "But so many of them have moved away or are too busy preparing for the holidays to socialize. I'm glad I was able to attend this event tonight. Maybe I can connect with some new people."

Sloane's Cheshire-cat grin widened. "Speaking of this event, how did you find out about it? Through your friend Todd?"

"No, actually. An old friend from high school. Rachel Bennett. You may know of her."

"Oh, yes. Rachel Bennett. The Museum of Contemporary Art's curator. I do know of her. We've actually met several times. I've invited Rachel to tea on numerous occasions. But she's a very busy woman. Unfortunately, we haven't been able to connect. Yet..."

"I may be able to help you with that," Elle said while filling out her bid sheet.

"That would be lovely."

The women were interrupted when a man walked over and tapped Sloane on the shoulder.

"My apologies for the interruption, ladies. Mrs. Whitlock, our chairman would like for the board of directors to join him onstage."

"Thank you, Fredrick. I'll be there in a moment."

Sloane reached inside her black Judith Leiber clutch and pulled out a business card.

"It was very nice meeting you, Elle. I'm hosting a private event at my home next week and would love for you to attend. My phone number is on the card. Call me. I'll share the details then. Feel free to invite Rachel, as well."

"That is so nice of you, Sloane. Thank you. I'll be in touch."

"By the way," Sloane whispered, "don't spend all of that extra cash you mentioned here at the auction. I've got a lucrative opportunity that'll provide a hell of a lot more than anything you'll find here."

She gave Elle a wink, then slunk off. The other women hurried behind her.

"Um, what just happened?" Elle asked Todd.

"Looks to me like your introduction to Sloane and The Precious Jewels was a success. That's what happened."

She clinked her glass against his. "We came. We saw. We conquered. I can't believe I got an invitation to one of their events that quickly."

"Of course you did. You're amazing."

The spark in Todd's eye told Elle he wasn't just referring to her investigative acumen.

"Thank you. Now that our work here is done, why don't we head over to our table and relax?"

Todd held out his arm. "Let me lead the way. I've been looking forward all day to that $250 filet mignon they're serving up."

Elle took his arm and together they walked across the room. "You know what? For the first time since arriving in Bradford, I feel good. I'm getting inside information from Rachel, we've got Bryce on our radar and now I'm in with The Precious Jewels. We're getting closer to finding out what really happened to Taylor."

Todd gave her arm a squeeze. "Yes, we are. And I cannot thank you enough."

"I keep telling you. You don't have to thank me. Taylor meant a lot to me, too. There's no place I'd rather be than here with you, working this case."

Todd stopped at the edge of the dance floor and kissed Elle softly on her cheek. "I appreciate you."

"Same. Now, before I burst into tears, let's do our best to enjoy the rest of the evening."

"Deal."

Chapter Seven

Todd peered around the corner. Sheriff Glover's office lights were out. It was almost 7:00 p.m. Todd assumed he'd gone home for the evening.

There were several deputies scattered around the station, either talking among themselves or focused on their computer screens.

Todd slipped inside the evidence room and closed the door behind him.

Earlier that afternoon, he'd seen a digital file in the department's database titled River Birch Park. There were no documents attached. Todd was determined to find the paperwork connected to the file, considering it was the location where Taylor's body had been found.

During the day, the evidence room was monitored, but after hours, whoever was on shift was supposed to keep an eye on anyone going in and out. The other deputies hadn't seen him slip in.

The evidence room's aisles were arranged in alphabetical order. He peered up at the signs, stopping when he reached the lane marked P-R.

Todd scanned the row of boxes containing files beginning with the letter R. When he tried to grab the first one on the shelf, it jammed between two others.

He gave it a good yank. Several boxes went crashing to the floor.

"What the hell was that?" a deputy yelled from the main floor.

Dammit!

Todd froze, praying no one would come back and investigate the noise. Several moments passed. No one showed up.

Thank you.

He eyed the mess he'd made. Files were scattered everywhere. Paperwork had spilled out of several of them.

Todd kneeled and began shoving documents back inside the folders, making sure to keep a lookout for the River Birch Park file.

"One box down, three more to go," he said while placing it back on the shelf. He bent down to refill another when his cell phone rang.

The volume was still turned all the way up from earlier that morning, when he'd been at the gym.

Todd jumped up and snatched the phone from his back pocket. He fumbled with the buttons until the ringing ceased.

"Dude, pull it together," he muttered to himself. "Deputy Jacobson speaking."

"Hey, it's Elle. You got a minute?"

He hesitated. "I do, but I've gotta make it quick. What's up?"

"I just spoke with Sloane. She extended an official invitation to a gathering at her house tomorrow evening. I think it's going to be some sort of Precious Jewels informational. Either way, I'll be there with my checkbook, ready to sign up."

"Excellent. I'm actually in the evidence room right now. I found a digital file labeled River Birch Park that didn't have any docs attached, so I'm trying to find the actual papers."

"River Birch Park, huh. Interesting. Why would the documents be missing? Is someone trying to hide something?"

"Maybe," Todd said. "If they are, I'm determined to find it. I'll search this place all night if I have to."

"Good. I'll let you get back to it. I have to call Rachel and beg her to attend this event with me. You know how she feels about The Precious Jewels. But since this is really a ruse that's for a good cause, I'm hoping she'll agree to it."

Todd stooped back down and shoved more files inside a box. "I'm sure she will. Let me know what she says."

"Keep me posted on your end, too. Let me know if you find anything."

"You got it. Talk soon."

As soon as Todd disconnected the call, he saw a file labeled RBP. He grabbed it and shuffled through the contents.

A white envelope slipped out and fell to the floor. Todd picked it up. The envelope was sealed. He hesitated, then tore it open.

A piece of paper was folded neatly inside. It contained a stack of photographs. The first two were images of the River Birch Park's hiking trail. The third was a picture of a massive tulip tree. It looked to be the exact same tree near where Taylor's body had been discovered.

Todd's hands shook as he shuffled through the photos. They appeared to be duplicates of those he'd already seen.

He reached the last pictures, then gasped. His muscles froze as the stack of photos hit the floor.

Todd fell back against the shelf. The cold metal edge dug into his back. He couldn't feel the pain. He was too numb.

He slid to the floor, forcing himself to look at the photo. The gruesome image of a woman's dead body, sprawled out underneath the tulip tree, glared back at him.

It wasn't Taylor.

Flashbacks of his sister's body lying in that very same spot flooded his mind.

"Stop it," he muttered, rubbing his head vigorously in hopes of wiping away the memory.

Todd flipped the picture over. He grabbed the file and shuffled through its contents. The sheriff's death scene report was stuck against the back of a coffee-stained list of evidence collected.

He pulled the papers apart and began reading the report.

The victim's name was Harper Mitchell. Her body had been found on the River Birch Park's hiking trail a little over a year ago. The manner of death was marked accidental. The cause of death—a broken cervical vertebra.

A fractured neck.

Todd slammed the report down and grabbed his phone, frantically dialing Elle's number.

"Hey," she said.

"You're not gonna believe this."

"Not gonna believe what?"

"Another woman died on the same hiking trail where Taylor's body was found."

The other end of the line went silent.

"Elle? Are you still there? Can you hear me?"

"I—I'm here. And I heard you. I'm just...*shocked*. Who is the woman?"

"Her name is Harper Mitchell. Does that ring a bell?"

"No, it doesn't. What happened to her? Is the cause of death listed?"

"Are you sitting down?"

"Uh-oh."

"A broken neck."

"Oh my God," Elle moaned. "What in the world are we dealing with here? Some sort of serial killer?"

"We could be. At this point, I'm not ruling anything out. What concerns me is that I never heard anything about this case. I was still on active duty when Harper died, so I was away from Bradford. But I don't like the fact that no one has mentioned this possible connection to Taylor's death. The cases are so similar. But the department just swept it under the rug."

"It sounds like the report had been hidden away on purpose. Those documents should have been attached to the digital file. Why weren't they?"

Todd flipped through the death scene report. "Good question. I don't know. We need to find out who Harper Mitchell is and what she had going on at the time of her death."

Todd could hear Elle typing away on her keyboard. The tension in his pounding head suddenly eased up.

"Already putting together a master plan, huh?" he asked.

"Of course."

"I've said this before, and I'll say it again. I am so glad to have you on my team."

"And I'm glad to be on it. Now, why don't you make a copy of Harper's file, and I'll contact Rachel to find out if she knows anything about her?"

"Good idea. I'll run a background check on her, too. See what comes up. And on that note, I'd better get the hell out of the evidence room before somebody sees me and I get hit with a bunch of questions."

"Be careful, Todd."

"I will."

Chapter Eight

Sloane stood in front of her Victorian-style great room's bay window, next to the massive Fraser fir Christmas tree. She ran her hands down her cream tweed dress then tapped her fingernail against a champagne glass.

"Ladies, if I could please have your attention."

The chatter ceased immediately. A jazz quartet playing their rendition of "Let It Snow" out in the foyer stopped the music.

Elle and Rachel sat down on a pewter silk love seat positioned near the back of the room.

"First of all," Sloane said, "I'd like to thank everyone for being here today. To all of the new faces in the crowd, welcome. And to those of you who are already members of The Precious Jewels family, welcome back. I'm hoping that our new attendees have had an opportunity to meet their assigned mentors and learn more about our illustrious organization."

"What assigned mentors?" Elle whispered to Rachel.

"I have no idea. I guess we weren't given one."

Elle felt a tap on her shoulder. She spun around and watched as a woman she'd never seen before tiptoed around the love seat and sat down next to her.

"Sorry I'm late," the woman murmured. She gave

Elle and Rachel a quick once-over. "I'm Chloe Hale. Your mentor."

"Oh, we were just wondering about that," Elle said, scooting over as the woman continued inspecting them.

Elle was glad she and Rachel wore almost identical navy wool suits. Judging by Chloe's intense scrutiny, appearance was a priority in her book.

"It's nice to meet you. I'm Elle Scott, and this is my friend Rachel Bennett."

Chloe slid forward and waved. "Yes, Rachel and I know one another well. She recently curated a friend's art show at the museum. I'm surprised to see her here. I've invited her to numerous events, but she's always turned me down."

"Hmm..." Elle gave Chloe a polite smile, watching as she pulled her long, honey-blond hair over her shoulder.

Chloe appeared to be in her mid-thirties and was quite beautiful. A violet sheath dress hung from her petite frame. Her porcelain skin was covered in very little makeup. Just a dusting of pale pink blush over her high cheekbones and a layer of sheer lip gloss.

"If anyone has questions," Sloane continued from the front of the room, "please feel free to speak with me or any of our other members. In the meantime, continue to enjoy the Christmas jazz quartet along with the hors d'oeuvres and cocktails."

Sloane rushed over to Elle as soon as she was done speaking.

"Hello! I'm so glad you could make it. And, Rachel, thank you for joining us. As you know, you're high on the list of Precious Jewels' potential members."

"So I've heard," Rachel replied through clenched teeth.

Elle discreetly nudged her arm.

"But I'm so happy to have finally found the time to attend an event," Rachel continued, sweetly this time. "From what I've gathered, it's a wonderful organization."

"Why, thank you. That means a lot, coming from someone as impressive as you. I've assigned Chloe as a mentor for both you and Elle. You'll be under the tutelage of one of our finest members. Chloe, have you had a chance to tell these ladies about The Precious Jewels and all of its great benefits?"

"Not yet. I arrived a bit late. But I'm planning to do so right now."

"Excellent. I'll leave you three to it. Elle, Rachel, be sure to see me before you leave."

"Thank you again for having us."

Chloe took a sip of her cranberry-orange mimosa. "Listen, ladies, I'm going to give you the real scoop on The Precious Jewels. This organization is amazing. It's filled with wealthy, accomplished women who have provided me with endless networking opportunities. The social aspects are great, too. These women know how to throw a party. And then there are the generous charitable contributions. So heartfelt, and so satisfying." She held her hand to the side of her mouth and added, "Not to mention they're a nice tax write-off."

"That all sounds fantastic," Elle said.

"Trust me, it is. But that's not even the best part."

"Ooh, there's more?" Rachel asked.

Her tone dripped with sarcasm. Elle resisted the urge to give her another nudge.

"Yes," Chloe breathed. "Much more. The Precious Jewels also offers its members an opportunity to generate a nice stream of residual income. But as they say, you have to pay to play. Entry into The Precious Jewels will cost you."

"How much, exactly?" Elle asked.

"Five thousand dollars."

Elle reached over and pinched Rachel's thigh before she could say a word.

"And in order to gain membership, you're required to bring in at least one recruit. That's how the organization grows and builds what we call the treasure chest."

Chloe drained her glass. "So, does that sound like something you two would be interested in?"

Elle reached inside her purse and pulled out her checkbook. "Yes, it certainly does." She turned to Rachel. "And you'll join with me as my recruit?"

"I sure will."

"Yay!" Chloe squealed, frantically clapping her hands. "So, here's a quick breakdown of how all this works. You ready?"

"Ready," Elle replied enthusiastically while Rachel followed with a lackluster "Yep."

"Okay, so Elle, once your membership is accepted, you and Rachel will be initiated into The Precious Jewels and considered what we call Sapphires. As you recruit new members, and your recruits bring in new members, you'll climb up the pyramid, going from Sapphires to Emeralds, then Rubies, and finally, *Diamonds*. Once you reach Diamond status? That's when you'll become eligible to cash out on your investment and receive the $150,000 treasure chest."

"Wow," Rachel uttered. "That's a lot of money. What is your current status?"

"Right now I'm back to being a Sapphire."

"Really?" Elle asked. "How is that? Haven't you been a member of the organization long enough to have reached a higher status?"

Chloe smiled stiffly. "Let's step out onto the deck. Where we'll have a little more privacy."

She stood and strolled through the great room. Elle and Rachel threw one another inquisitive looks before following her.

On the way to the kitchen, Chloe was stopped by a fellow group member. As they chatted, Elle tugged Rachel's sleeve.

"Hey," she whispered, "I've been meaning to ask, were you able to find anything out about Harper Mitchell?"

"Oh, yes! I was so caught up in trying to get here on time that I forgot to mention it. My sister was familiar with Harper because she banked at Bradford Financial. Harper was originally from North Carolina, but traveled back and forth between here and Florida for her husband's job. Then she filed for divorce and got her own place in Bradford. Harper shared that she was expecting a generous settlement. But she died before the divorce was finalized."

"Oh, wow. That's interesting. I wonder if Todd received the results on her background check. They may be delayed since she was living state to state—"

Elle stopped abruptly when Chloe walked back over.

"My apologies for the interruption, ladies. Please, follow me."

She led them through a luxurious all-white kitchen out onto the deck.

"This yard is beautiful," Elle said, eyeing the vast area. Sparkling icicle lights hung from the tall bamboo privacy fence. Bright blue viburnum shrubs and yellow winter jasmine plants surrounded a stunning gazebo. Solar fairy lights filled the deck's glass lanterns.

"Please, have a seat," Chloe said, pointing toward a set of sleek beige lounging chairs. "There are some things I'd like to share with you both. First of all, to answer your questions, Elle, I did in fact reach Diamond status not too long ago. Then I cashed out on my investment and received the treasure chest. After that happened, I dropped back down to Sapphire status and started the process all over again. That's how the income cycle works."

"*Okay,*" Rachel said slowly. "Why would you need privacy to tell us that? Isn't it known knowledge among the members of the group?"

Chloe looked away and began fiddling with her platinum tennis bracelet. "It is. But the way that I attained the treasure chest was somewhat controversial."

"Why is that?" Elle asked.

"Because… Taylor Jacobson was my mentor."

Elle gripped the arms on her chair.

Don't say a word. Just let her finish.

"Taylor was the one who recruited me into The Precious Jewels. I came in with her, just like Rachel is coming in with you, Elle. Taylor should have collected the treasure chest instead of me. She'd worked *so* hard to get there, too…"

Chloe's voice trailed off.

"It's okay," Elle told her. "Please, go on."

"I'm not sure how much you two know. But...um... Taylor was out for a run one afternoon and stumbled on the hiking trail. She fell and broke her neck. I still can't believe she's gone."

Chloe dropped her head. Tears trickled down her cheeks, streaking her pale pink blush. "And that's how I collected the treasure chest. It was really Taylor's money. She should still be here, enjoying her earnings."

"She really should," Rachel interjected. "How unfortunate that she isn't."

Sloane appeared in the doorway. "Excuse me, ladies. I'm sorry to interrupt, but we're ready to begin the initiation process. Elle, Rachel, are you two prepared to become official members of The Precious Jewels?"

"Yes, we are," Elle said, quickly dabbing at her damp eyes.

"Wonderful!" Sloane pressed her hands together. "Once we're done, we'll all celebrate over Veuve Clicquot and eggnog crème brûlée. I'll meet you ladies in the living room in a moment. Chloe, could you please join me and the other Precious Jewels in the dining room?"

"Yes, of course."

Elle and Rachel hung back on the deck while the women went inside the house.

"I do not have a good feeling about these women, Elle. Especially this Chloe chick. There's something sinister going on here. I can literally feel the underlying current of greed, jealousy and superficiality running through this entire operation."

"So can I. Isn't it interesting that Taylor died right before she was set to collect that treasure chest?"

"Of course it is! It took everything in me not to dig

deeper and interrogate Chloe. *Taylor stumbled on the trail.* Girl, please…"

The two friends slowly walked back inside the house.

"I'm glad you didn't interrogate her," Elle said. "We've got to remain low-key and play the game. Not show our hand. Maintain that poker face of yours while we infiltrate this group and get some answers."

ELLE'S CELL PHONE buzzed on the way home from Sloane's house. She stopped at a red light and swiped open her home screen.

A text message from Sloane appeared.

Thank you again for attending our event, and welcome to The Precious Jewels! Remember, ladies, discretion is key. What goes on within our organization stays within our organization. Please do not share any information with anyone. That goes for husbands, family members and friends alike. Again, welcome to the club. You're going to love it here. All my best, Sloane Whitlock

A horn blasted behind Elle. She looked up, realizing that the light had turned green.

Elle hit the accelerator and sped down the dark road. She approached a stop sign and glanced in the rearview mirror. The car that had blared its horn came careening toward her.

"Stop!" Elle screamed just as the driver slammed on the brakes inches away from her bumper.

The vehicle's screeching tires pierced her ears. Its headlights flooded inside her car.

She was triggered.

Elle squeezed the steering wheel, twisting her palms along the smooth leather.

This cannot be happening again...

She glanced to her right. Bright lights shone down on Green Avenue, illuminating the shiny new cars parked throughout the Capital Motors lot.

Elle made an abrupt turn down the street and prayed that the looming vehicle wouldn't follow her.

She sped toward the dealership, quickly glancing in the rearview mirror. The car's engine roared. It peeled off and kept straight.

"Thank God." Elle sighed, pressing her hand against her heaving chest.

She let up on the accelerator. All of the lights were out inside the dealership's offices. It was already after eight o'clock. Business was closed.

Elle stared up at the surveillance cameras positioned throughout the lot. Several of them hung from the pole lights. As she drove closer toward the sales office, Elle noticed cameras lining the corners and center of the roof's edge.

Todd had yet to retrieve surveillance footage from the day Taylor died. Bryce's movements were still unknown. While they waited, Elle figured it would be helpful to know where the cameras were positioned throughout the dealership.

She parked her car along the side street and stepped out. The cool night air was still. And unnervingly silent.

Elle pulled her phone out of her beige trench coat and shuffled toward the lot. Her thin high heels skidded along the grainy asphalt. She wished she'd brought a more comfortable pair of shoes.

But who knew I'd be participating in an impromptu assignment?

Elle climbed through the metal railing and snapped several photos of the sales office's surveillance cameras.

Just as she turned to take pictures of the ones hanging from the pole lights, a pair of headlights appeared.

They crept toward her. Elle tried to get a better look at the vehicle, but she couldn't. The side street was too dark.

Make this quick, then get the hell out of here.

She walked to the back of the lot. Stood in the middle of an aisle and aimed her phone up toward the pole light.

An engine roared loudly.

Elle spun around. A black pickup truck sped into the lot. It resembled the one that had crashed into her at the forest preserve.

No. No. No!

She tried to jump in between a row of cars. But she couldn't move. Her legs were laden with fear.

The truck raced toward her. Elle screamed, unable to budge.

Come on. Come on. Move!

She closed her eyes and braced herself.

This is it. This is how I'm going to die...

She opened her eyes. The pickup was a few feet away from her.

"Stop!" she screamed.

Right before the truck made impact, the driver swerved around Elle.

The passenger door brushed up against her body.

Elle fell to the ground and rolled over, clutching her arm in agony.

Get up. Get up!

She attempted to stand. But her legs were too weak. She dragged her body in between two cars. The rough concrete scraped against her bare legs. Elle ignored the pain and focused on getting to safety.

The truck circled the lot. It sped up, then slowed down, then sped up again, like a predator tormenting its prey.

Elle struggled to get a look at the license plate. But there were none mounted on the front or back.

"Please leave me alone," she pleaded. "*Please* leave me alone…"

The driver gunned the engine. Elle recoiled, sliding further in between the cars.

My phone!

She held up her cell, anxiously waiting for the facial recognition to register.

The pickup truck flew around the corner and raced down the aisle where Elle was hiding.

"Come on. *Activate!*" she yelled at the screen.

The truck came to a screeching halt right in front of Elle's hiding spot. She looked up at the black tinted windows, straining to peer inside.

Her phone rang. She jumped at the shrill chime.

Anonymous Caller.

Elle looked back up. She had a feeling that the call was coming from inside the truck.

She tapped the accept button.

"Yes?" she whispered.

"Ah, you answered."

A cold chill seeped through her skin. It was that

voice. That deep, creepy, cartoonish voice of the person who'd called the night of the charity gala.

Be strong. Don't back down...

"Who the hell are you? What do you want?"

"First things first. Are you okay? Or did you scar those gorgeous legs of yours when you fell to the ground?"

"I'm fine. Is your truck okay? Or did I dent it when you hit me? Unfair advantage, using a pickup as a weapon. Why don't you step out and show your face?"

"Oh, you would love that, now, wouldn't you? But no. I'll pass. By the way, I'm the only one making demands tonight. My advice to you? Stop your little investigation and go back to New York before you get yourself killed. Because next time I see you? I won't spare your life like I did tonight."

Elle thought about Taylor. A surge of courage shot through her. She jumped up and ran toward the truck.

"Get out!" she yelled, slamming her hands against the window. "Get out and show your face, you coward!"

The driver revved the engine. Smoke billowed from the tailpipe and surrounded Elle. She choked, barely able to see through the thick fumes.

The truck sped off. Elle stumbled backward, wincing as the rear tire grazed the tip of her shoe.

She struggled to stay on her feet. "You *maniac*!" she hollered.

Elle whimpered as she limped back to her car. She finally unlocked her phone and dialed Todd's number. It went straight to voice mail.

"Todd," she moaned, "I've been attacked again. Meet me at my parents' house as soon as you get this message."

Chapter Nine

"I don't know how much more of this I can take, Todd."

"Come on, Elle. You can do this. *We* can do this. Don't give up on me now."

The pair were sitting on his backyard's Asian-inspired heated deck. Several days had passed since her attack, and she was still shaken up.

Todd had hoped that inviting Elle over for grilled Cajun shrimp and sausage kebabs would help lift her spirits.

She did seem to appreciate the fresh orchid arrangement that served as the centerpiece, the slim bamboo waterfall gurgling softly in the corner and the stone lanterns shining brightly along the yard's pathway. But despite the soothing ambience, Elle still appeared frazzled.

She pulled her wringing hands apart long enough to refill their glasses with Chablis.

"Don't get me wrong," she began. "I'm not saying that I'm giving up. But I *am* getting tired. Law enforcement can't seem to find my attacker, who's doing an excellent job of finding me. I'm still mad over the shoddy investigation into Taylor's death. Then we find out that a similar death occurred in the exact same location almost a year to the day Taylor died. I feel like that case was deliberately kept from you. I mean, what's really going on with our sheriff's department? Is it just sloppy work or something else?"

"I have no idea. But you're absolutely right. Seems like we can't catch a break. I still haven't heard back from Dr. Wu on whether or not he's reached out to Sheriff Glover. I'll call his office again tomorrow morning and see if I can get through to him."

"What about the surveillance from the car dealership? Any luck in contacting someone about footage from the day Taylor died and the night I was attacked?"

Todd shook his head. "I'm so sorry, Elle. I've been waiting for the right time to tell you that all of the footage was taped over before anyone had a chance to review it."

"On both occasions?"

"Yes."

"Ugh!" Elle groaned. "How the hell did that happen? And how did you find out?"

"Deputy Cross knows a security guard who works at the dealership. I talked him into reaching out and asking for his help. The guard admitted that the staff is very lackadaisical when it comes to reviewing the surveillance. You already know the sheriff's department never requested footage from the day Taylor died. As for the night you were attacked, by the time it was ordered, it had already been recorded over."

Elle dropped her head in her hand. "I feel like we're fighting a losing battle here."

"Come on, E. Don't give up hope. Trust me. We will get to the bottom of all this. It's just gonna take some time. Don't forget, you and I are going at it alone. We don't have the power of law enforcement behind us. But we're still a force. We can do this."

She looked up, her expression softening. He reached over and squeezed her hand.

"You're right," she said. "We can do this. I won't give up."

"That's my girl." He paused, slowly releasing her hand. "Listen, there's something else I need to say."

"I'm listening," Elle said before plucking a shrimp off a bamboo skewer and popping it inside her mouth.

"I don't want you going out on any more of these solo missions. It's too dangerous. I could've easily gone to the dealership with you to take photos of the cameras."

"I know. But it was a last-minute decision that I made on a whim."

"Which is even more dangerous, Elle. Trying to pull off an unplanned operation like that just isn't wise. Especially now that you know someone is following you. You've got to be more careful. I need to keep a closer eye on you, too."

She gave him a salute. "Sir, yes, sir. I hear you, Deputy Jacobson. Loud and clear."

"Oh, so you're gonna go all formal on me now? Don't tease me, woman. I'm being serious."

"I know you are. I'm just being respectful of your orders. But anyway, what's going on with Harper's background check? Any updates?"

"I reached out to a former marine buddy of mine who works for Miami-Dade County Corrections Department. He's gonna run the checks on Harper and her estranged husband. See if anything comes up since they were spending a lot of time in Florida. I'm hoping to hear from him by the end of the week."

"If anything substantial comes back, would you feel comfortable presenting that plus all of the other evidence we've collected to Sheriff Glover in hopes that he'll reopen Taylor's case? Even without Dr. Wu's recommendation?"

"I most certainly would."

"Good." Elle reclined in her bronze wicker chair and stared out at Todd's ranch-style home, which he'd inherited once his parents moved into a nearby retirement community. "You know, it feels good being back here. I spent so many years running around this yard, playing with Taylor and the rest of our little crew."

"Yeah, I remember those days well. Life was good back then, wasn't it?"

"It really was…"

Elle's expression fell as her downturned lips began to tremble.

Say something. Anything!

"You know," Todd said, "there is one thing that's missing around here."

"What's that?"

"Christmas decorations."

Elle sat up and looked around. "I hadn't even noticed. This house used to be the most festive on the block. Your parents went all out during the holiday season. What did they do with all those ornaments?"

"They're still here, tucked away in one of the spare bedroom closets. I thought about setting them out, just to brighten up the place. But this year, I haven't been in the merriest of moods. For obvious reasons."

"Of course. Neither have I."

Todd drank the last of his wine, then stood. "I have an idea."

"And what might that be?"

"Why don't we decorate the place? I mean, we don't have to go all out like my parents did. Maybe just put a few things up. I kept the faux Fraser fir stored in the basement. All of the lights, ornaments and wreaths are boxed up inside that closet I mentioned. And I was gonna save this for later, but, I went to Cozy's this afternoon and picked up some gingerbread hot chocolate and butter snowflake cookies for dessert."

A slight smile crept across Elle's lips. "Are you really trying to seduce me with Gigi's delicious desserts in order to get your house decorated?"

"Ha! I might be. Is it working?"

The pair burst out laughing.

"Whatever your intentions are," Elle said, "they worked." She picked up her plate and glass. "Come on. Let's clear these dishes and get to work."

"Yes, ma'am."

Todd's body felt lighter as he followed Elle inside the house. While they were both grieving the loss of Taylor, having Elle there was certainly making the process much easier.

TODD CRACKED OPEN a plastic container filled with silver bells, crystal icicles and iridescent snowflake ornaments.

"Ooh, these are gorgeous," Elle breathed.

"Taylor and my mom handpicked all of those." He stood back and crossed his arms over his chest. "We're doing a hell of a job on this tree, aren't we?"

"We are. It looks stunning."

"I'm sure you remember how much Taylor loved Christmas. You hadn't been home for the holidays in years, so you never attended one of her tree trimming parties. She'd host two of them. One at her place, and one here. That woman went all out for both, too. She handpicked most of these orname—"

Todd's voice broke. He closed his eyes. "I still can't believe she's gone," he whispered.

Elle wrapped her arms around him. Her soft, warm touch eased the strain running through his tense shoulder blades.

"I know," she said. "I can't believe it, either. But look at us, cherishing her memory by continuing her tradition. How ecstatic would Taylor be knowing that we're celebrating the season together and hanging her decorations?"

"She'd love it."

Elle grabbed their mugs of hot chocolate and handed one to Todd. "Gigi really outdid herself with the holiday treats this year."

"Yes, she did," he replied, appreciating her attempt to lighten the mood.

"I think I ate about six of those butter cookies."

"That's okay." His eyes roamed Elle's body. Her curves were accentuated in a fitted mint green sweater and black leather leggings. "You look great. A few cookies won't hurt. Plus, it's the holidays. Calories don't count during this time of year, remember?"

She bent down and pulled a snowflake from the container. "I wish that little joke of mine was true. Try telling it to my waistline."

A warm sensation stirred below his black leather

belt. Todd turned away and took a gulp of hot chocolate, burning his tongue in the process.

"Once we hang this box of ornaments," Elle said, "I think that's it. There won't be an inch of free space left on this tree."

Todd grabbed a handful of silver bells. He approached the tree just as Elle spun around. Her breasts brushed up against his chest.

She jumped back, almost falling into the tree. Todd caught her just in time.

"Ooh!" Elle squealed, clutching his shoulders. "I am so sorry. I wasn't paying attention and didn't see you coming when I—"

"Hey, calm down. It's okay. The tree is still standing and we're both fine."

Her hands drifted from his shoulders to his forearms. "Thanks. I need to relax. I freaked out imagining this gorgeous tree crashing to the floor."

"We'd just have to pick it up and start all over again."

Todd felt drawn to Elle's vulnerability. It was a side of her that he rarely saw. She was always so tough.

"So you're good?" he asked.

"I think so. Just a little flustered. Maybe I drank too much wine..."

"Or maybe it's me," he boldly suggested.

Their mouths were inches apart. Todd could smell the sweet scent of gingerbread on her breath.

Go for it...

He gently pulled her toward him. Their lips lightly touched, and he waited, silently asking for permission. Within seconds, the kiss intensified. All of Todd's worries melted into that moment.

His cell phone buzzed inside his pocket. They both jumped back, startled by the vibration.

"I am so sorry," he panted, digging for it. "Just give me a minute."

Elle's hands fell to her sides. "No worries."

He could hear the disappointment in her tone. The disruption made him want to punch a hole in the wall.

"This is Jacobson," he barked into the phone as Elle fiddled with a miniature snow globe.

"What's up, Todd? This is Ryan. Listen, I got the results on those background checks you requested."

Todd signaled Elle over and put the call on speaker.

"Really? That was fast. What'd you find out?"

"Harper's came back clean. But her ex-husband, Keaton? Not so much. He was arrested for domestic violence and disorderly conduct early last year."

"Were there any details attached to the charges?"

"There were. According to the report, Keaton violated the order of protection that Harper had taken out on him while they were in the middle of their divorce proceedings. He showed up at her place of residence. A struggle ensued, and he allegedly tried to strangle her. A neighbor saw what was going on and called the authorities."

"Damn," Elle whispered. She grabbed her phone and began taking notes.

"Did law enforcement note Keaton's motive behind the attack?" Todd asked.

"They did. According to Harper, he was angry over the divorce settlement."

"Got it. Thanks, Ryan. That'll definitely give us something to work with. Would you mind emailing that report to me?"

"Make sure he sends it to your personal email address," Elle whispered.

Todd gave her a thumbs-up.

"I'll text you my personal email address. You can send it there."

"Will do. If you need anything else on my end, just give me a holler, brother. Oorah."

"Oorah."

Todd disconnected the call. He and Elle stared at each other in disbelief.

"Unreal," Todd uttered. "On one hand, we've uncovered a possible motive behind Harper's death. But on the other hand, if her estranged husband murdered her, that wouldn't have anything to do with Taylor's case."

"Right. But how weird is it that their bodies were found in the exact same location and their causes of death matched?"

"It's very weird."

"This case is getting more and more twisted by the day." Elle glanced at her watch. "It's getting late. I should probably get going."

Todd hesitated. He was hoping they would pick up where they'd left off before Ryan's call. Clearly the mood had shifted. At least for Elle.

"Okay," he muttered reluctantly. "Let me get you home."

"Thank you again for dinner. And dessert. And the impromptu tree trimming party."

"The pleasure was all mine," Todd said, wishing the night didn't have to end.

Chapter Ten

Sloane approached the portable cherrywood podium positioned in the front of her great room and banged her gavel against the sound block. "Ladies, please. Let's settle down. I'd like to call this meeting to order."

The room fell silent.

"Good morning. Welcome to The Precious Jewels' sisterly sit-down. I'd like to extend an especially warm welcome to all of our new members."

A round of applause ensued. Seasoned Jewels smiled and waved at the newbies. Elle and Rachel nodded their heads politely.

"Ew, this is so phony," Rachel mumbled through her stiff grin.

"Just play the role and remember that it's only temporary."

"Now," Sloane said, "let me start by saying how proud I am of our group's growth. We have recently initiated several outstanding women into our distinguished organization. Our recruitment efforts have afforded us endless opportunities. Whether you're looking to enhance your social circle, charitable footprint or financial status, The Precious Jewels can turn those goals into a reality."

Elle heard someone sitting behind her snort loudly.

"Yeah, speak for yourself, sweetie," the woman muttered.

Elle glanced over her shoulder. A slender brunette with a spiked pixie haircut and face full of chalky makeup was slouched down in her chair, picking at her bright red acrylic nails.

"While we may all have different objectives in mind," Sloane continued, "there is one thing that each and every one of us cherishes. And that is our *sisterhood*. What do I mean by sisterhood?" She stepped away from the podium and walked around the room. "I mean bonding. Providing support for one another. Being a shoulder to lean on. Cry on. Whatever our fellow Jewel may need at any given moment."

"Are you kidding me with this crap?" the brunette ranted under her breath.

Rachel nudged Elle's arm. "Whoever this woman is sitting behind us, we need to talk to her."

"Mmm-hmm," Elle agreed, keeping her eyes glued to Sloane.

"For those of you who have moved to the next levels toward that treasure chest, congratulations. And for those of you whose movement has stalled, don't give up. Keep working hard to recruit new members. If you're having trouble doing so, book a training session with one of our highly skilled recruitment specialists who can help you—"

Sloane was interrupted when the brunette burst out cackling. "Yeah, and how much is that session gonna cost us?"

Sloane stopped in the middle of the floor. "Sara, we

have not yet reached our Q and A segment. Once we do, feel free to ask any questions that you may have. But until then, please respect those who are speaking. Thank you."

"Whatever. *Little Miss High-and-Mighty...*"

Sloane threw her a look before continuing. "As I was saying, if you're having trouble recruiting new members, schedule a meeting with one of our specialists. Their track records speak for themselves."

A woman sitting near the bay window waved her hand in the air. "I don't mean to toot my own horn or anything, but *beep beep*!"

Everyone laughed and applauded.

"That's right, Linda!" Sloane exclaimed. "You deserve to toot that horn of yours. You are one of our top recruitment experts. And I've got the receipts to prove it!"

"Oh, so that bitch can interrupt Queen Sloane," Sara grumbled, "but I can't. Got it."

The room fell silent. Sloane cleared her throat.

"Linda, could you please make the big announcement about our fellow Jewel, Michelle? I need to speak with Sara privately."

"Yes, of course."

Linda jumped up and hurried toward the podium while Sloane marched over to Sara. On the way there, she stopped in front of Elle and Rachel. "Ladies, I am so sorry for the rude interruption. Trust me, this is not a normal occurrence." She glared at Sara. "Nor will it ever be."

"You don't have to apologize on my behalf," Sara shot back. "Just give me back my initiation fee since I'm never gonna cash in on it. What do I have to do? Join your little circle of flunkies over there?" She pointed toward the group of women who'd attended the charity gala with Sloane. "*That'll* never happen. I refuse to kiss your—"

"Sara!" Sloane interrupted. "In the kitchen. Now!"

Sara jumped out of her seat and stormed off.

"Lord, please help me not strangle this woman," Sloane whispered under her breath before going after her.

Elle and Rachel elbowed one another. The room buzzed with hushed chatter.

Linda pounded the gavel.

"Ladies, please! Let's all settle down and get back to the business at hand. We're supposed to be celebrating Michelle Ingram's promotion to Diamond status. Woot woot!"

Linda burst into applause. Her glossy orange lips spread into an exaggerated, joker-like smile.

The rest of the women slowly followed suit, still reeling from Sara's outburst.

"Congratulations, Michelle," Linda continued. "We are all *thrilled* that you're next in line to receive the treasure chest. Now, why don't we take a break and enjoy the cocktails and hors d'oeuvres until Sloane returns?"

Linda stepped away from the podium, her smile quickly fading as she rushed toward the kitchen.

"Girl!" Elle whispered to Rachel, "what have we gotten ourselves into?"

"I have no clue. But had I known The Precious Jewels were this entertaining, I would've joined a long time ago."

"Can you believe Sloane said something about strangling Sara?"

Elle cocked her head to the side. "That was an interesting choice of words. Trust that I made note of it, too."

ELLE AND RACHEL teetered down Sloane's winding driveway, holding on to one another so as to not topple over in their five-inch pumps. When they reached the curb, Sara waved at them from across the street.

"Hey! You two got a sec?"

"We sure do," Rachel replied, grabbing Elle's hand and shuffling over the asphalt.

Sara took a long pull from her cigarette, then leaned against a run-down gray sedan. "You all look nice."

"Thanks, so do you," Elle lied, eyeing her ill-fitting mustard suit and beat-up ballet flats.

Sara tugged at her blazer's tattered hemline. "You, um, you don't remember me, do you?"

Elle squinted, then shook her head. "Your face looks a bit familiar, but no. Have we met?"

"Sort of. We went to high school together. I was a few years behind you. And…let's just say we didn't run in the same circles, if you know what I mean."

"Oh…okay." Elle opened and closed the flap on her tan suede clutch, racking her brain for a subject change.

"So, Sara," Rachel said, "how did you end up becoming a member of The Precious Jewels?"

"Ha!" Sara chortled. "Good question. I know what you're thinking. I know I don't fit in with these hoity-toity bitches. But I needed some money. *Bad.* I met this really cool chick who promised she could help me make some quick cash. So, like a fool, I believed her. I did what she suggested, took out a second mortgage on my house and joined the group."

"I heard you mention that you haven't earned any money back on your initiation fee," Elle said.

Sara blew a stream of smoke in the air, then tossed her cigarette butt. "Nope. I haven't. And honestly, how could I? Everybody I know is just as broke as I am. I haven't been able to recruit a single soul into this shady-ass pyramid scheme. And Sloane refuses to refund my money so I can just quit altogether. So basically, I'm screwed. Do you all know my husband would kill me if he found out about the second mortgage? Which is why I have got to get my money back. I wish—"

Sara paused. Her eyes glazed over.

"You wish what?" Rachel asked softly.

"I wish the woman who recruited me was still around. She's the one who got me into this mess. Too bad she can't help get me out of it."

"Who recruited you?" Elle asked.

"Taylor Jacobson."

Elle's stomach dropped.

"She died not too long ago." Sara pointed at Elle. "Wait, weren't you two pretty tight? Seems like I remember you all hanging out a lot during high school."

Elle swallowed the lump of grief creeping up her throat. "Yes. We were."

"Sorry for your loss," Sara muttered.

"How did Taylor convince you to join The Precious Jewels?" Rachel asked.

"Funny story. I was at Capital Motors trying to buy a car. Taylor just so happened to be there, getting chewed out by her husband for whatever reason."

Rachel coughed lightly. Elle threw her a look. The comment hadn't gone over either of their heads.

"Taylor heard that I didn't get approved for a loan,

so she chased me down on my way out and told me about this so-called money-making opportunity that would change my life."

Sara paused. She pulled another cigarette out of her pocket and lit it. "If only I knew then what I know now. I would've turned that woman down immediately. This mess has me so stressed out that I started smoking again after quitting three years ago."

"Bye, ladies!" Elle heard someone call out.

She looked up.

Chloe drove by in a silver Range Rover, performing her best beauty pageant wave. "See you all next week!"

Elle and Rachel waved back.

Sara rolled her eyes and flicked her cigarette ashes. "I'd better get out of here. I've gotta pick my husband up from work. We're down to one car, and unfortunately, it's this piece of junk."

"Thanks for being so open with us," Elle said. "I'm looking forward to hearing more of your story."

"No problem. I'm like an open book. As you can see, I don't hold back. With that being said, I'd watch out for that Chloe chick if I were you two. I know she's your little mentor and all, but I don't like her."

"Why not?" Rachel asked. "She seems cool."

Sara wrapped her thin lips around the tip of her cigarette and took a long pull. "I just don't trust her. That whole caring, sugary-sweet act is as fake as Santa Claus. Chloe is all about money. She'll do anything to get it. And I do mean anything."

Elle peered over at Rachel, her brows creased with curiosity.

"Has she done anything illegal that you know of?" Rachel asked.

Sara threw her head back and laughed. "Girl, this whole damn operation is illegal. But that's a conversation for another day. For now, I'll just say that it's awfully coincidental how Taylor died right before she was set to receive the treasure chest. And who got the money instead? *Chloe*."

"Well, coincidence could be all that there is to it," Elle debated.

"Yeah, okay. Maybe that argument would hold up better if the same situation hadn't happened before."

Elle almost dropped her purse. "What do you mean, if it hadn't happened before?"

"Oh, you sweet, innocent newbie. You two don't even know the half of it. The woman who recruited Taylor into The Precious Jewels died right before she was set to receive the treasure chest. Since Taylor and Chloe were next in line to reach Diamond status, they ended up splitting the money. Then, when the rotation came back around, and Taylor had reached Diamond status again, she died right before she could collect. Who received the money instead? *Chloe*."

"Wait," Rachel said, "we never heard about another death being linked to The Precious Jewels."

"Of course you didn't. The women in this organization are powerful. And well-connected. Whatever they want swept under the rug *stays* under the rug."

Sara's cell phone buzzed.

"Dammit. That's my husband texting me. We both work down at the meat processing plant and he took my shift so I could attend this meeting. I was supposed to pick him up twenty minutes ago. I gotta go."

She handed Elle her phone. "Here. Add your number. There's a lot more I wanna share with you two."

"Thanks," she said, taking the phone and adding her info. "We'd appreciate that. It'll be good for us to know both sides of The Precious Jewels."

"Both sides? Uh-uh. There's only one side to this. And it ain't good. If I had time, I'd tell you all about how Sloane and Taylor fell out right before Taylor died."

"Excuse me?" Rachel said.

"Look, this situation runs way deeper than you know. Sloane had pretty much cut Taylor off a couple of weeks before her body was found."

"Why?" Elle asked. "Wasn't Taylor one of The Precious Jewels' biggest recruiters? What could she have possibly done to make Sloane that mad?"

Sara's lips curled into a smirk. "That's the problem. Taylor became *too* good of a recruiter."

"That doesn't even make sense. The Precious Jewels are all about bringing in as many members as possible. More members, more money. Right?"

"Right. But in Taylor's case—"

Sara was interrupted when her cell phone buzzed again.

"Listen, I've got to get outta here. Call me. We'll get together somewhere far away from the prying eyes of these women, and I'll tell you everything I know."

She climbed inside the car and attempted to start her engine. It sputtered loudly, then stalled. She punched the steering wheel.

"*Man*, I need a new car! Come on. Not now. Come on!"

Sara turned the key and pressed down on the accelerator. After two more attempts, it finally started.

"Wait!" Elle said right before Sara closed the door. "Before you go, tell us. Who was the other member of The Precious Jewels who died?"

"Her name was Harper. Harper Mitchell."

Chapter Eleven

Todd strolled inside the sheriff's department with Taylor's evidence file tucked securely under his arm.

Be cool. Be confident. Kill!

He ran the Marine Corps motto through his head over and over again on the way to Sheriff Glover's office.

"Good morning, guys," he said to a group of deputies huddled near the break room. "How's everybody doing?"

The men ignored him and continued chatting among themselves.

Todd stopped and turned around. "I said good morning."

A couple of them grumbled something inaudible while the others sipped from their coffee cups, barely looking at him.

Todd waved them off and kept it moving.

He approached Sheriff Glover's office, took a deep breath then knocked on the door.

"Come in!"

Todd stuck his head inside. The sheriff's normally cluttered desk appeared neat and tidy. It was a good sign. Maybe he wasn't too busy for an impromptu chat.

"Good morning, boss. You got a minute?"

He glanced up from his laptop. The handsome, six-four, former Ironman triathlon champion looked more like a professional athlete than a law enforcement officer.

Framed photographs of him crossing finish lines at triathlons around the world hung from the walls, next to certificates of achievement and pictures with various dignitaries.

"Jacobson," he growled, his full lips twisting into a slight snarl. "Just the man I need to see. Have a seat."

Todd's legs grew heavy with apprehension as he sat down. "You need to see me? What's going on?"

Sheriff Glover ran his hand along his salt-and-pepper goatee. "You tell me. I got a call from the medical examiner's office this morning."

"Really? That's great. So what did you think of Dr. Wu's—"

"That's great? No. That's *not* great. What in the hell would possess you to go behind my back and meet with the coroner? About a closed case that you didn't even work on, no less?"

"I can explain—"

"Hold on. Before you do that, let me say this. I understand that Taylor was your sister. I can only imagine how painful her death has been for you and your family. You're frustrated. You want answers that make sense to *you*. But you have got to respect our department's investigative process and final reporting on the matter."

Todd's knee bounced rapidly. *"On the matter,"* he repeated. "Meaning my sister's death." He stared down at the thin gray carpeting, struggling to choose his words wisely.

"Sheriff Glover, I do respect the department's final

reporting. I just don't agree with it. And it's not that I'm studying this case through an emotional lens. Nor a personal one. I'm taking an objective look at the evidence. According to it, we are not dealing with an accidental death here."

Todd's chest swelled with hope when Sheriff Glover sat back and nodded his head.

I've got him. He's hearing me out. Keep going.

"According to Dr. Wu's findings," Todd continued, "Taylor's neck injury could've been caused by manual strangulation rather than an accidental fall. That fractured ankle? It was severe. That plus the muddy footprint left on her sock proves someone may have stomped Taylor's—"

The sheriff held up his hand. "Son, let me stop you right there. First of all, Dr. Wu wasn't able to fully present his findings to me because he called during the middle of my deputies' meeting."

"Did the deputies happen to hear your conversation with him?"

"Yes. They did."

"Interesting. I guess that explains the collective cold shoulder they gave me when I walked in this morning."

"Well, can you blame them? These guys don't like being second-guessed, Jacobson. Especially by a rookie. You think an attacker caused Taylor's neck and ankle injuries? Where's the proof? I can't reopen this case based on a muddy sock. My deputies didn't uncover one shred of physical evidence from that hiking trail proving another person was involved."

Maybe that's because the attacker outsmarted your deputies...

"Not only that," the sheriff continued, "but our former medical examiner, who'd been on the job for over forty years, declared Taylor's death an accident. That just confirmed our team of investigators got it right."

Todd bit the inside of his cheek and pulled out Elle's report on The Precious Jewels. "Have you heard of this organization?"

Sheriff Glover slipped on his black-rimmed glasses and flipped through the pages. "Yeah, I have. It's some sort of social club. A few of the members attend my church. Why?"

"Taylor was a member of the group. It's way more than just a social club. It's actually a pyramid scheme."

Todd waited for the sheriff to say something. He responded by closing the report.

Keep pressing...

"There's a lot of money being funneled through this organization, Sheriff Glover. And it's causing problems among the members. Major problems. There's jealousy, infighting, backbiting—"

The sheriff snickered. "Sounds a lot like game night at my house."

Todd showed no signs of being amused.

"Listen, Jacobson. I'm familiar with these women. They're just a bunch of bored, superficial housewives who don't have anything better to do than to sit around gossiping and eating crumpets. They're harmless."

"Harmless? I'm sorry, sir. But I have to respect-fully disagree." Todd pulled out the notes he'd taken on Harper Mitchell's death. "Taylor isn't the only per-son linked to The Precious Jewels who's dead. Do you remember the case of Harp—"

Todd was interrupted by a knock at the door.

Please tell whoever it is to come back later.

"Come in!" the sheriff called out instead.

Major Dixon cracked open the door. Todd acknowledged him with a wave. Dixon ignored him.

"I'm sorry to interrupt, Sheriff. But we've got the video call set up in the conference room. Our virtual briefing with the mayor starts in five minutes."

"Thanks. I'll be there in a second."

Sheriff Glover pulled a brush out of his drawer and ran it over his short dark hair. "Look, son. If I were you, I'd keep my head down and focus on my current workload. Again, I'm sorry for your loss. But there just isn't enough evidence here to justify reopening Taylor's case."

"I appreciate that, sir. But you didn't even give me a chance to finish presenting what I've—"

The sheriff stood. Todd knew what that meant. The meeting was over.

"Do me a favor, Jacobson. Don't go behind my back and pull another rogue stunt like this again. You're a former marine. You know loyalty. Give this department the same amount of respect you gave your infantry brothers."

"Yes, sir."

Todd's skin burned with anger. He shoved the evidence back inside the folder, forcing himself to stand tall on his way out the door.

SHERIFF GLOVER HEADED to the conference room while Todd made a beeline toward his desk. Fellow law enforcement officers glared at him. A disgruntled buzz floated through the air.

Todd blocked it all out. He didn't care if the entire

department turned against him. If getting justice for his sister meant ruffling his colleagues' feathers, so be it.

He collapsed into his chair and pulled out his cell phone. A text message from Elle appeared.

Good morning! Excited for your meeting with Sheriff Glover. Let me know how it went as soon as you get a chance!

Todd hit the reply button so hard that he almost cracked the screen.

Went horribly. Dr. Wu called Sheriff Glover this morning and the sheriff shut us both down. The rest of the department caught wind of the situation and they've iced me out. We need to come up with another course of action.

He sent the message. Within seconds, the cell rang. It was Elle.

Todd spun around in his chair, making sure no one was hovering near his desk.

"Hey," he murmured in the phone.

"Hey, I know it's probably easier for you to text since you're at the station. But I was so shocked when I saw your response that I had to call. I'm sorry you got shut down and are being ostracized like that."

"Yeah, it's unfortunate. But I'm tough. I can handle it. My number one concern is Taylor. I'm still all in on our investigation."

"So am I. As far as taking another course of action is concerned, I've already got one. You know that defiant member of The Precious Jewels I was telling you about, Sara?"

"The one with the beat-up car who took out a second mortgage on her house behind her husband's back?"

"Yes. Her. She invited Rachel and me to some retro country music bar for a line dancing event tonight. Rachel can't go because she's hosting an opening at the museum. I asked if I could bring you instead. Sara was a little hesitant at first."

Todd ran his fingertips along the lines in his forehead. "Really? Why?"

"Because you're a deputy sheriff. And the crowd she runs with doesn't usually associate with law enforcement. But I convinced her that you're cool and just looking for some answers."

"All right. So, am I in?"

"Yes. You're in."

Todd opened his laptop and pulled up the internet. "What's the name of the bar?"

"BB's Two Step."

"Hmm. Never heard of it." He entered the name in the search engine. A distressed wooden shack popped up on the screen. "Ooh, this place looks pretty rundown. More like an oversize outhouse than a bar."

"Ew," Elle uttered. "Where exactly is it located?"

"Right outside of Bradford, in Old Creek. Not my usual stomping grounds, that's for sure."

"Mine, either. It's a pretty rough area. But we're not going for the ambience. This is about business. We can step out of our comfort zone for one night if it means getting a new lead on Taylor's case."

"True. What time do we need to be there?"

"Around eight p.m."

"All right, cool. I'll pick you up at seven fifteen—"

Todd paused when a couple of deputies walked past his desk.

"Sellout," one of them muttered in his direction.

Todd jumped up from his chair. The deputies stopped and turned around.

"Is there a problem?" one of them asked.

"I don't know," Todd shot back. "You tell me. Is there?"

"Nah, man. We're good. You good?"

"I most certainly am."

The men stared each other down for several moments. When Todd didn't back down, the deputies shook their heads and walked away.

"What is going on?" Elle asked.

"Looks like I'm being challenged by my fellow law enforcement officers." Todd slowly sat back down. "These dudes have no idea. I'm just getting started. And I won't stop until I get justice for my sister."

"Neither will I. Keep your head up. If nobody else has your back, you know I do."

"Thanks, Elle. I appreciate that."

"Deputy Sheriff Jacobson!"

Todd almost dropped the phone. He spun around in his chair. Sheriff Glover was standing directly behind him.

"Yes, sir?"

"It is nine forty-five a.m. You were supposed to be in the conference room for the crisis intervention training session fifteen minutes ago."

"I'm on my way, sir."

"Uh-oh," Elle said. "Sounds like I'd better let you go."

"Definitely. I'll see you tonight."

Chapter Twelve

"Ooh," Elle breathed. "This place is worse than I thought it'd be."

"I couldn't agree with you more."

Todd led Elle inside BB's Two Step. It took her eyes a minute to adjust to the darkness as she searched for Sara.

The stench of stale beer filled the smoky air. Shania Twain's "Any Man of Mine" blared from the speakers. Peanut shells crunched underneath the soles of Elle's black riding boots. The atmosphere was a far cry from her normal social scene.

She noticed Todd bobbing his head to the beat of the music.

"Already enjoying yourself, huh?" she asked.

He shrugged and cracked a sexy smile. "Hey, what can I say? I like Shania's music."

Elle's gaze traveled down to Todd's hips as they rocked back and forth in his slim-cut jeans. Her mind drifted to that kiss they'd shared in front of his Christmas tree. She wondered what it would've led to had they not been interrupted by his cell phone.

Stop it, she thought before quickly turning away.

"Do you see Sara anywhere?" Todd asked.

"I don't. But she texted me saying that she's here. We should do a lap and find her."

"Let's do it." Todd placed his hand on the small of her back. "Why don't we stop by the bar first and grab a drink, then look for her?"

"Sounds good. I'd love a vodka tonic."

"One vodka tonic, coming right up."

Patrons threw them strange looks as they walked by. Elle pulled her fitted denim jacket over her black bodysuit, covering the cleavage peeking over her top's neckline.

"Two of these kids do not belong," Todd sang in her ear.

His soft lips nipped at her earlobe. Elle ignored the tingles that shot down her neck. "Yep. It's pretty clear that we're not members of BB's clique."

A woman at the other end of the bar waved her arms in the air.

"Elle! *Elle!*" Sara yelled while dancing toward them. "Hey, you two made it!"

"Hey, yes, we did."

Sara's ruby red-lips were spread into a bright smile. She was dressed in an army green tank top and skinny jeans that were ripped at the knees. Her dark brown cowboy hat matched her dusty steel-toe boots.

She held her arms out at her sides and spun around. "See, I'm in my element here. Not at some stuffy ass Precious Jewels meeting. Now you'll get the *real* me." Sara took a step toward Todd and held her hand in the air. "Nice to meet you. Elle says you're cool, so I'll break my cardinal rule and hang out with law enforcement for a night."

He gave her a high five. "Why, I'm honored. Thank you. Can I get you a drink?"

"No, thanks. I've already had three beers and two rum and Cokes. I'd better pace myself. Come on. Grab your cocktails and let's go over to my table so we can talk."

They trailed Sara through the throng of plaid shirts and cowboy boots. She led them to a high-top table near the edge of the dance floor.

"Sara!" someone yelled as they sat down on rickety wooden stools. "Get your ass out here! This is our favorite song."

"Gimme a minute! I've got some business to tend to."

Sara drained a half-empty bottle of beer that was sitting on the table. Her eyes darted back and forth between Elle and Todd. She threw her head back and laughed.

"Clearly this place isn't your thing, huh?"

Elle smiled sheepishly. "I mean…it's fine. I'd never even heard of it until you mentioned meeting up here."

Sara tipped her hat at Todd. "What about you, Bradford's finest? Have you been here before?"

"No, I haven't. But it's cool. I may have to hit the dance floor and try my hand at that two step they're doing out there."

"Yes!" Sara exclaimed. "You should. First things first, though. My girl Elle here wants to know what I know about your sister, Taylor. I'm sorry for your loss."

"Thanks. I appreciate that."

"So, Sara," Elle said. "You mentioned that Taylor and Sloane fell out right before Taylor died. What exactly happened between them?"

"Long story short, Sloane felt like Taylor was recruiting a lower caliber of women into The Precious

Jewels than she wanted. I'm sure I was included in that
mix. You know Sloane and her *image*. But, whatever.
Bottom line is Taylor was all about quantity. That girl
was trying to collect as much money as she could.
Sloane, on the other hand, was all about *quality*, i.e.
fake, bougie women."

"And Sloane confronted Taylor about all this?" Todd
asked.

"She sure did. During one of our meetings, right in
front of all those *lower caliber women* that she didn't
want in the group. They were so offended. I was the
only one who spoke up, along with Taylor. Everybody
else was either too intimidated or blind to the fact that
Sloane was referring to them."

Elle sipped her drink, mulling over this new information. "What happened after the big fallout?"

"All hell broke loose, that's what happened."

"Meaning?" Todd asked.

"Meaning The Precious Jewels started to crumble.
It got so bad that Taylor decided to launch her own
group. She secretly approached a lot of fellow Jewels
asking if they'd leave Sloane's organization and join
hers. Everybody knew Taylor was pulling in a lot of
money. She was a hustler. So most of them said yes."

Todd held up his hand. "Wait a minute. I thought
The Precious Jewels were about sisterhood. And charity. And female empowerment. Where was that whole
philosophy in all this?"

Sara threw her head back and laughed. "That's all a
farce, man. The Precious Jewels are all about money,
status and more money. Period. That's why so many
members were willing to run off with Taylor. She
was making some major promises. A real sisterhood

with better money-making opportunities, in a relaxed, judgment-free zone."

Sara paused. She grabbed the napkin from underneath her beer bottle and pressed it against her eyes.

"Take a minute if you need it," Elle said.

As she waited for Sara to regroup, something dawned on her. Taylor's notebook. That last paragraph in the journal entry that had left her so confused.

I am going to press on toward the goal. Collect the treasure chest. Then move on to bigger and better things...

Maybe Taylor's plan to launch her own group was that bigger and better thing. And it ended up getting her killed.

"You look like something's on your mind," Sara said to Elle. "What is it?"

Keep it to yourself. At least for now. You still don't know who's played what part in all this...

"Oh, nothing. I was just waiting on you to finish your point. Please. Go ahead."

"Taylor was just getting started. She had some great ideas. She and one of her recruits named Audrey decided to name the new group The Blossoms. Each tier would be represented by a different flower. Once you reached rose status, you'd cash out on the garden, which was equivalent to The Precious Jewels' treasure chest. But none of that ever happened..."

Sara's voice trailed off. She sniffled inside of her napkin.

"Audrey, Audrey..." Elle murmured, tapping her fingernails against the table. "That name doesn't ring a bell. Was she at the last meeting?"

"No. She's no longer a member of the group. Audrey and Taylor were really close. Like, best friends. When Taylor died, Audrey was too distraught to stay on board. So she left. I really miss her, too. She was a super cool chick."

Todd pulled out his cell phone and scrolled through the contacts. "I've never heard Taylor mention anyone named Audrey. I have most of her friends' numbers, too."

"She hasn't been in Bradford for that long. Audrey moved here when she got a job at the car dealership where Taylor's husband works. That's how she and Taylor met." Sara wiped away the stream of black mascara that had trickled down her cheek. "But anyway, back to shady Sloane. I can't let her win, guys. I wanna see her get locked up for whatever role she played in Taylor's death."

"So you think Sloane had something to do with this?" Elle asked.

"You bet your ass I do. You have no idea how... how *arrogant* that woman is. Imagine someone like that being dethroned by a member of a group that *she* started. Trust me, Sloane wasn't gonna let Taylor ruin her reputation by dismantling her organization. So yeah, I believe she fought to the death before that could happen."

A somber silence fell over the table. Elle felt the urge to get up and leave the bar.

"All right, ladies and gents!" the DJ yelled into the mic. "It's time for my favorite part of the evening."

Melodic guitar chords blasted through the speakers. The crowd went wild. A sea of cowboy hats and boots bum-rushed the dance floor.

"Tonight's cowboy cha-cha is being sponsored by

one of my favorite duos, Brooks & Dunn," the DJ continued. "It's time to hit the floor and get to spinning to the tune of their greatest hit, 'Neon Moon.'"

A tall, slender man dressed in all black came two-stepping toward their table. He spun around in front of Sara, then held out his hand.

"May I have this dance, darlin'?"

"Not now, Pete. I'm in the middle of something here."

He sized up Elle and Todd, his beady eyes narrowing.

"Aw, come on, Sara," he pressed. "This is your favorite song. Plus your husband's not here tonight, which means you're free to dance with me." Pete nodded his long, narrow head in Elle and Todd's direction. "You don't look too happy sittin' over here with these two anyway. What do you say? Just one dance? And maybe one drink afterward?"

Sara hesitated.

"I do love this song…"

"Go on," Elle told her. "Enjoy yourself. You probably need a break from us anyway."

"Are you sure?"

"Positive," Todd chimed in. "I think we could all use a quick break."

"Yeehaw!" Pete howled through a snaggletoothed grin. He grabbed Sara by the waist and helped her off the stool, then practically carried her onto the dance floor.

"I'm glad Sara's husband isn't here," Elle said.

"If he were, I doubt that Pete would've even approached the table." Todd threw his head back and drained his bottle of beer. "What do you think of that info Sara just shared?"

"It was pretty insightful. Especially the new intel on Taylor and Sloane's relationship. You know, the more I learn about this situation, the more I realize just how much Taylor was keeping from me."

"Yeah, me, too. Even though I'm her big brother, she was usually open about what was going on in her life. But she kept all this to herself."

"Which tells me she knew it was wrong and didn't want either of us calling her out on it."

"Hey, Elle! Todd!" Sara yelled from the dance floor. "Come on out here and get your cowboy cha-cha on with us!"

Todd extended his hand. "What do you say, cowgirl? Should we take a shot at this cha-cha thing?"

Elle watched as Sara and Pete took three steps forward, rocked back, did a half turn and cha-cha-cha'd to the side.

"And make a complete fool of myself in front of all these people?" she asked. "I think I'll pass."

"Oh, please. You know how to do the Electric Slide, don't you? This isn't much different. Come on. Let's give it a try."

Todd didn't give Elle a chance to respond. He grabbed her hand and pulled her onto the dance floor.

"There they are!" Sara exclaimed. "All right, y'all. Show us what you're working with."

Elle shuffled her feet, stumbling about as she tried to keep up with Sara and Pete.

Todd caught on right away. When Elle almost fell into him, he grabbed her hips until her steps matched his.

"There you go," he said. "You got it."

His hips pressed against hers as they stepped from

side to side. A tingling heat crept up Elle's thighs. She considered pulling away from him, but he was holding on to her too tightly.

Just relax and enjoy yourself...

Sara shuffled over to Elle and twirled around her. "You know what I forgot to mention?"

"What's that?"

"As much as I can't stand Sloane, I think Taylor's shady-ass husband could've had something to do with her death."

"What makes you think that?"

"Well, thanks to Chloe, practically every Precious Jewel knew that Taylor and her husband were having marital problems. Taylor thought Chloe was her friend. She confided in her about how she'd taken out the second mortgage on the house behind Bryce's back, ran up their credit cards buying all those designer clothes and purses. I wouldn't be surprised if he got fed up and offed her."

"Interesting theory," Elle said, not letting on that she and Todd shared the same sentiment.

"Motive!" Sara yelled, pointing over at Todd. "I learned all about that watching true crime shows on the Investigation Discovery channel. If Bryce did do it, he had a *motive*. Right, Sergeant?"

"You got it," Todd said, giving her a thumbs-up while throwing Elle a look.

"Ladies and gentlemen," the DJ shouted over the music, "you all are killing this one! The bartender wants me to remind you that drinks jump to full price in ten minutes. When you're done cha-cha sliding, head over to the bar and show Katt and her crew some love. Tell 'em I sent you, and don't forget to tip!"

Pete tapped Sara on the shoulder. "Let's go grab a drink before the prices go up."

"Let's do it!" Sara turned to Elle. "I'm gonna get a beer. Wanna reconvene after that?"

"I'm actually pretty tired. My days of partying are long gone. Why don't we make plans to get together again sometime soon?"

"Yes, please! And in the meantime, if I think of anything else you need to know, I'll reach out."

Pete grabbed Sara's arm. "We'd better hurry up. The bar is getting crowded."

"Bye, guys!" she yelled, waving wildly before rushing off.

The DJ switched things up and threw on a love song. Couples headed to the dance floor as the cowboy cha-cha-ers departed.

Todd took Elle's hand and led her through the crowd toward the exit. "You're not too tired to come by my place for a nightcap, are you?"

That tingling in Elle's thighs shot straight up to her chest. "No. I'm not."

"Good. Because I've got an amazing bottle of rosé that I've been dying to pop open. Tonight seems like the perfect evening to do it."

"It does. The night was a success. We accomplished what we came here to do. So yes. Let's toast to our progress."

Todd gripped Elle's hand a little tighter as they stepped outside.

Through the corners of her eyes, she noticed a flash of silver speed out of the parking lot.

Tires screeched. The stench of rubber filled the air.

Elle caught a glimpse of a silver truck before it disappeared behind a convenient store.

Was that Chloe's Range Rover?

"What's wrong?" Todd asked her. "You look like you just saw a ghost."

"I—I actually think I just saw…" Elle paused. "Wait!"

She took off running toward the parking lot's entrance. Stared down the street.

The truck was gone. Its only trace was the squeal of shredding tread.

Todd ran over.

"Elle! What is going on? Did you see something?"

Did I?

"I—I thought I did."

"What was it?"

Elle's head spun with uncertainty. She didn't want to appear paranoid. So she lied.

"No. I didn't see anything. There's just so much going on. I guess my mind is playing tricks on me."

"What is it that you *thought* you—"

"Don't even worry about it," she interrupted, locking her arm in his. "Let's just go back to your place and enjoy that rosé."

Chapter Thirteen

Elle took a sip of her sparkling wine. The fruity bubbles lingered on her tongue. She swallowed slowly, watching as Todd lit the firepit out on his deck.

His biceps flexed underneath his fitted green shirt. Elle crossed her tingling legs, willing the heat, which had never quite gone away, to simmer down.

"How's the wine?" Todd asked.

"Delicious, as promised." Elle reached for a cube of cheddar cheese and popped it inside her mouth.

"And the charcuterie board? How'd I do with that?"

"You did amazing," she said, eyeing the large wooden round filled with cured meats, various cheeses, dried fruits and crackers. "Who knew the former quarterback turned decorated marine turned deputy sheriff could whip up such a fancy display."

"Hey, what can I say? I'm a man of many talents."

The light from the firepit's flame glowed against Todd's handsome face. He grabbed a chair and pulled it closer to Elle's than necessary. When he reached for his glass, his arm brushed up against hers. His touch warmed her skin.

He tapped his glass against hers.

"Are we toasting to something?" she asked.

"We are. To us getting that much closer to solving Taylor's case. Thanks to Sara, I think we've got a pretty solid new lead."

"I agree. Sloane has risen to the top of the suspects list. But what about Bryce? Do you still think he may have been involved?"

"Oh, absolutely. Bryce is still on the list. So is your mentor, Chloe. Honestly, and this may surprise you, so is Sara."

Elle's head fell to the side. "*Sara?* Even after tonight? She's doing so much to help us."

"Maybe that's her tactic. To try and throw us off by offering up her assistance. As long as she's pointing the finger at somebody else, we'll be too occupied to look at her. Right?"

"Possibility. She does have a motive. Sara's pissed about the initiation fee that she can't get back. Deep down, I think she blames Taylor."

Todd emitted a low groan. He slowly piled slices of prosciutto and smoked gouda onto a rosemary cracker, hesitating before taking a bite.

"You know, our parents didn't raise us to be materialistic. And self-serving. Taylor had to have known that Sara couldn't afford to be a part of The Precious Jewels and keep up with the recruiting demand."

"That's why I believe Sara felt used. It was as if Taylor recruited her just to elevate to the next level, knowing she wouldn't be able to follow suit. Sara was destined to fail."

The loaded cracker Todd had been holding fell onto the plate. "I wish I'd known about all this. If I had, Taylor would still be alive. I'd have sensed the trouble brewing and insisted she walk away."

A vein pulsated down the middle of Todd's forehead. Elle reached out and clasped his hand. "Do not blame this on yourself. Taylor chose to keep us both in the dark for a reason. All we can do now is try and figure out what happened to her."

"You're right," he whispered, intertwining his fingers within hers.

They sat silently. Despite their worry over Taylor's death, Elle was overcome by a calming sense of peace. Being in Todd's presence helped ease the burden of grief.

She inhaled. The cool night aired rushed through her lungs, clearing her mind.

Elle sat back and stared up at the sky. Twinkling stars shone against the velvety dark blue sky. There was one that sparkled brighter than the others. She observed its glimmering rhythm, feeling Taylor's presence in the glow.

"We're going to solve this case, Todd. Don't lose faith."

His grip on her hand tightened. She turned to him, surprised by the soft, hopeful expression on his face. The creases in his forehead had faded. His mouth was no longer twisted into a scowl.

"I won't lose faith," he declared. "With you by my side, how could I? Together we can do anything."

Todd's words shot straight through Elle's chest and penetrated her heart. Waves of heat settled into her skin. As streams of smoke floated through the air, she knew it wasn't the crackling firepit causing her body to burn. It was him.

He slid toward her. She leaned in. Their bodies pressed against each other's. Her lips parted.

Bang!

Elle jolted forward. Todd fell back so fast that he almost toppled out of his chair.

"What the…"

Bang! Bang!

They stood and stared up at the sky.

"Are those fireworks?" she asked.

The only thing flashing up above was the stars.

"What is that noise—"

Todd stopped abruptly at the sound of smashing glass.

"Gunshot!" he yelled. *"Get down!"*

Todd grabbed Elle and pulled her underneath the table. He covered her body with his as shots continued to ring out.

She clung to him, flinching with every blast of the gun.

"Sounds like somebody's shooting inside my living room. Where the hell is my cell phone?"

"I think you left it inside the house."

Todd frantically patted down his blue jean pockets. "I did. It's on the kitchen counter. Right next to my Glock. Dammit!"

Elle's head swiveled from right to left. "My phone is out here somewhere. I think I left it on the table."

Todd reached up to grab it.

Bang! Bang!

"Wait!" she shrieked. "Just leave it. No phone call is worth you getting shot over."

He hunkered back down underneath the table.

Elle's limbs trembled with terror. Todd wrapped his arm around her tightly. "Come on. I got you."

"What if the shooter comes back here?"

"I've got the backyard's security gate locked. By

the time he gets through it, we'll be back inside the house." He paused. "Wait. Listen..."

Silence filled the air. Then police sirens blared in the distance.

Elle gripped her chest, releasing a heavy sigh. "Thank God. One of your neighbors must have called the police."

"Good. Maybe now the department will start taking this entire situation more seriously."

A blaring engine revved loudly.

Elle froze. She recognized that roar.

The black pickup truck!

"Todd!" she screamed. "That's my attacker! They must've followed me here."

"What makes you think that?"

"I'd know the sound of that engine anywhere. Trust me. The person who's been after me just shot up your house."

The sirens drew nearer. Brakes screeched out front.

"This is the sheriff's department," someone yelled over the loudspeaker. "Deputy Jacobson, are you home?"

"We're in the back!" he called out. "Is the coast clear?"

"We're surveying the scene now. Stay put. We'll update you shortly."

Elle's cell phone buzzed against the glass tabletop.

"I should see who that is."

Todd ran his hand along the edge of the tabletop.

"Got it."

He handed the phone to Elle just as someone knocked on the fence.

"Deputy Jacobson? It's Deputy Cross. Are you all right?"

"Yes, we're fine."

"Looks like the coast is clear. Can you come and unlock the gate? Tell us what happened?"

Todd jumped up and ran to the front of the yard.

Elle was slow to stand. When she did, she fell against a chair. Her quivering legs were still weak with fear.

She sat down and willed her shaky hands to unlock her cell phone. A text message appeared from an unknown number.

Back off your investigation and get the hell out of town before you end up like Taylor!

The message sent a bolt of adrenaline straight through her.

Elle quickly rose to her feet and charged through the yard, anxious to show it to Todd.

Chapter Fourteen

Todd sat in the back of the sheriff department's conference room with his arms crossed over his chest and a scowl on his face. He was only half listening to the Force Option Training Unit's director, who was reviewing firearm and de-escalation techniques. Todd couldn't focus on anything except the attack on his home.

Who in the hell would have the audacity to shoot up my house?

It had been a week since the assault. While the sheriff's department hadn't produced any leads, Todd did notice a change in his colleagues' demeanor. The silent treatment and snubs were replaced with concern. Their "good mornings" and "how are things going" appeared genuine.

More importantly, the shooting proved that Todd wasn't being paranoid. He was on to something.

Todd's cell phone buzzed. It was Elle calling. He declined the call and sent her a text message.

Hey, can't talk right now. In a training session. What's up? Everything okay?

Everything's fine. Just checking on you and sharing some new intel. I spoke with Sara, and she brought up that woman Audrey whose name she'd mentioned at BB's. Remember her?

Todd hid his phone underneath the table so as not to get called out by the training director.

She's the one who was helping Taylor start up the new organization, right?

Right. Sara suggested we talk to her since she and Taylor were so close. Audrey knows all about the beef between Taylor and Sloane, and the issues Taylor was having with Bryce. What do you think?

Todd glanced around the room. The instructor was busy writing on the whiteboard while his colleagues took notes.

Sounds like Audrey could be an asset to our investigation. We should definitely talk to her. How do we get in touch?

Audrey's been off the grid since Taylor's death. If she's not at work, she's at home. Sara suggested we stop by her house tonight, introduce ourselves then go from there. Said she'd be happy to help figure out who killed her friend.

"Deputy Jacobson!" the director shouted from the front of the room.

Todd shot straight up. "Yes, sir?"

"What's got you so preoccupied that you can't focus on this whiteboard?"

"I was…um…"

"Could you please answer the question I just asked the group?"

A sheet of sweat formed along the back of Todd's neck.

The short, stocky director came strutting toward him. His bulky arms swung by his sides as if he were marching in a military parade.

Deputy Cross, who was sitting next to Todd, held his fist to his mouth and quickly muttered, *"Name one of the top gun safety rules."*

The director stood over Todd, heaving like a bull ready to storm a rodeo.

Todd's nose wrinkled at the stale stench of coffee on his breath. "Handle any weapon as if it were loaded, sir."

The trainer's narrow gray eyes darted back and forth between Todd and Deputy Cross.

"Good," he finally said. "Now get your head outta that phone and pay attention."

"Yes, sir."

As soon as he walked off, Todd turned to Cross. "Nice save. Thanks."

"Don't mention it. I know where your head's at. I hope you find the bastard that killed your sister."

The words almost knocked Todd out of his chair. It was the first time anyone in the department had shown him some support for his investigation.

"I appreciate that, man. I'm trying."

He sent one last text to Elle while the trainer's back was turned.

Gotta sign off. I'll pick you up at six and we'll head over to Audrey's.

TODD MADE A right turn onto Kenilworth Lane and let up on the accelerator. He turned on the windshield wipers, clearing a layer of foggy mist.

"We're a couple of blocks away from Taylor's house, aren't we?" Elle asked, peering out at charming cottage-style homes.

"Yep. Three to be exact."

The quaint residential street was filled with festive Christmas decorations. Streetlamps were wrapped in candy cane garland. Twinkling lights and wreaths adorned the entryway of each home. Children ran in between Santa and snowman figurines lining their perfectly manicured lawns.

Todd's chest pulled at the sight. He couldn't connect with all the merriment. His mind was focused solely on catching his sister's killer.

"You have arrived," the navigation system announced. "Your destination is on the right."

Todd parked in front of a dark gray vintage bungalow. A tall, slightly overweight woman dressed in black workout gear stood out front, wrapping string lights around the porch's white wooden railing.

"Here we go," Todd said. "Let's see what we can find out."

The woman he assumed was Audrey stared at them as they climbed out of the car. When the pair walked up the driveway, she froze.

"Uh-oh," Elle muttered. "Please don't freak out…"

The bundle of string lights fell from her hand. She tucked her honey-brown bob behind her ears, her dark, close-set eyes squinting curiously.

"Todd? Elle?"

They paused.

"I'm sorry," Elle said. "Have we met?"

"No. We haven't. I'm Audrey. A friend of Taylor's. And I could point you two out in a crowd. Taylor talked about you both incessantly. Between her scrolling through your social media and sharing stories about the good ole days, I feel like I've known you for years."

Her words warmed Todd's heart. "That's nice to hear. And it's good to meet you."

"You as well." She pointed at them. "Wait, let me guess. Sara sent you over here to check on me, didn't she?"

"She did," Elle replied. "She shared with us how close you and Taylor were, and how devastated you've been since her death."

"Elle and I were actually hoping you'd be willing to talk to us about what was going on in Taylor's life before she passed."

Audrey pressed her hands against the sides of her face. "Taylor was going through a lot. And I do mean *a lot*. But yes. Of course. I'll share with you everything I know. Hopefully it'll help get us closer to finding out what really happened to her."

"So you don't believe Taylor died from an accidental fall, either?" Todd asked.

"Absolutely not. Somebody wanted that woman dead. I think I know who it is. And I don't think that person acted alone."

Elle nudged Todd, her eyes gleaming with hope.

"We'd love to get your take on all this," he said. "Do you have time to sit down and speak with us now?"

Audrey looked at her watch. "I have to hop on a virtual therapy session in about thirty minutes. But please, come inside. I just made a pot of hot chocolate. We can have a quick cup and talk until my therapist calls."

"Great. Thank you."

The pair followed Audrey inside. Her contemporary, neutral-toned living room was packed with plastic bins, each of them stuffed with colorful Christmas decorations.

Audrey hurried over to the russet tweed sofa, snatched up several rolls of wrapping paper and propped them in a corner.

"Please excuse the mess. In case you couldn't tell, I've been drowning my grief in holiday decor. Have a seat. I'll go and get the hot chocolate."

Todd turned to Elle as soon as they sat down. "Who do you think is at the top of Audrey's list of suspects?"

"Sloane. Definitely Sloane. But she mentioned the suspect having help. I wonder who that could be."

"Maybe one of Sloane's cronies. I remember them from the charity gala. I get the impression that if Sloane told any of those women she wanted someone dead, they'd be begging to pull the trigger. But who knows. Audrey may surprise us and say she suspects Bryce."

Elle pulled out her cell phone and opened the Notes app. "We'll soon find out."

Audrey came back carrying a green ceramic tray topped with red mugs and a plate of gingerbread cookies. "I hope you two like whipped cream in your hot chocolate. I got overly excited that you're here and didn't even think to ask. Blame it on me not having company very often these days."

"All good," Todd said. "Elle and I both love whipped cream."

Audrey served the refreshments, then took a seat on an ottoman. "So, where should I start?"

"Wherever you feel most comfortable," Elle told her.

She stared down at her mug, her sunny disposition dimming. "I'm guessing you're both aware of Taylor's involvement in The Precious Jewels organization."

"We are. And we know that you and Taylor were in the process of leaving the group to start your own."

"We were. Actually, it was going to be Taylor's group. She was the driving force behind it all. I just acted as her wing woman. During that transitional phase, Taylor made quite a few enemies."

"Was that because she was working to pull members away from The Precious Jewels?" Todd asked. "Or was there more to it?"

"Oh, there was definitely more to it. Sloane was infuriated that Taylor had attempted to disband the organization she'd worked so hard to build. She wasn't the only one who was angry, though. A lot of Taylor's recruits were mad when she approached them about leaving the Jewels and joining her group, since they had yet to receive the money she'd promised they would earn."

Todd set his mug on the acrylic coffee table and rubbed his hands together. "Was Taylor expecting these recruits to pay another initiation fee in order to join her group as well?"

"She was. Needless to say, that didn't go over very well. And before we were able to come up with an amiable solution, Tay—"

Audrey paused. She held her hand to her mouth, sobbing softly.

"Taylor died."

Todd glanced down at the plate of cookies, quickly looking away when his stomach turned.

"I am so sorry, Audrey," Elle said softly. "I know this is hard for you considering how close you and Taylor had become. And I understand that there were a good number of people upset with her. But who would've wanted to take her life?"

"Sloane Whitlock."

"And you mentioned her having help," Todd interjected. "Who else do you think was involved?"

Another long pause.

He twisted his watch around his wrist, anxious to hear her response.

"Sara," Audrey whispered.

"I'm sorry, who?" Elle asked.

"Sara," she repeated, louder this time. "She was more upset with Taylor than anyone else. That money she put up to join The Precious Jewels was all she had. Sara realized she'd never cash in on her investment, and felt that Taylor stepped on her back to reach the next level. Most of Taylor's recruits felt that way. But it hit Sara the hardest. I don't think she could cope with the betrayal."

"I'm surprised at your response," Todd said.

"Why? You don't think that makes sense?"

"No, that's not it. I was under the impression that you and Sara were friends."

"When it comes to The Precious Jewels, there is no such thing as friends. Those women aren't trying to create genuine bonds. They're trying to make money and enhance their social status. That's why I was so willing to jump ship and join Taylor's group. Hers would've embodied a *real* sisterhood."

"So you don't think Taylor's husband had anything to do with her death?" Elle asked.

"*Bryce?* No. I mean, I knew he wasn't happy about Taylor's wild spending habits. But he loved her. Bryce wouldn't have harmed her over money issues—"

Audrey was interrupted when her laptop pinged.

"Oh, that's my therapist. Give me a quick sec," she said before jumping up and rushing into the dining room.

Todd rubbed his temples as his head began to throb. "I guess I'm not the only one who thinks Sara could be involved."

"I didn't see that one coming. This case just keeps getting more and more twisted."

"And the list of suspects keeps getting longer and longer."

The pair stood when Audrey returned.

"Thank you for speaking with us," Todd said, "and for being so open." He pulled a business card from his wallet and handed it to her. "If you think of anything else that might assist in our investigation, please don't hesitate to reach out."

"Thanks for stopping by and asking my opinion. I hope what I shared was helpful."

"It definitely was."

Audrey opened the door, her expression hardening. "Trust me. The truth behind Taylor's death is hidden within The Precious Jewels. Just be careful. Those women are dangerous."

"We'll keep that in mind," Todd said as he and Elle exited the house.

They headed to the car in silence. Audrey's ominous words ran through Todd's mind.

"That was pretty damn sobering."

"It was," Elle agreed. "We've got a lot to unpack. I think I'm gonna need to do so over something stronger than hot chocolate."

"Drinks at Cozy's?"

"Sounds good to me."

Todd opened the passenger door. Elle stepped off the curb, stopping before climbing inside the car.

She pressed her hand against his chest. "You were great in there. Keep it up. We're getting closer to the truth."

"Thanks, E. I hope so."

And just like that, Todd's somber mood lifted.

Chapter Fifteen

Elle adjusted the hem of her lavender cocktail dress and glanced around the room. The Museum of Contemporary Art was filled with the major players of Bradford, who'd come for the opening of an exhibition of works by North Carolina's own Pilar Samuels. Even the mayor had shown up to celebrate the artist, who had recently been featured at Art Basel in Miami.

As she wandered through the event, Elle's thoughts drifted to her evening at Cozy's with Todd. They'd talked about the case, but they had also enjoyed some much-needed laughs as they reminisced about growing up in Bradford. A smile crept to her lips as she thought of him squeezing her hand across the table, and the sweet kiss they'd shared at night's end.

Elle approached one of Pilar's sculptures. The life-size, all-black clay figure of a woman lying in the fetal position was depressing to say the least. The work wasn't Elle's cup of tea, but major curators from around the world seemed to love it.

"So, what do you think?" Rachel asked, handing Elle a glass of champagne. "Would you shell out six figures for this masterpiece?"

"Um, no, ma'am."

"Well, believe it or not, five of Pilar's pieces have already sold. I'm guessing the other three will sell before the end of the night."

"Good for her," Elle muttered, only half listening as she scanned the room once again.

Rachel had personally invited The Precious Jewels to the opening, along with Audrey, whom she'd met at a previous art exhibition. She and Elle were interested to see how they'd all interact with one another. Maybe hidden secrets would be unearthed and unspoken truths revealed once the champagne kicked in.

"Looks like Sloane and her cronies aren't here yet," Elle observed.

"Of course not. You know they like to make an entrance. Seems like they're a good hour late to every event they attend."

"They really think they're A-list celebrities, don't they?"

"Around here, they are," Rachel rebutted, smoothing the collar on her cream tuxedo dress. "The real housewives of Bradford."

The museum's heavy wooden doors opened. Elle stood on her tippy toes, peering over the heads of the sea of guests. Two unfamiliar faces entered the lobby.

"Ugh," Elle groaned. "None of our guests are here yet. They'd better show up. It took a lot of convincing for Audrey to agree to come. She doesn't even wanna be in the same room as The Precious Jewels. Especially Sloane. But I told her that seeing them might be therapeutic. All that hate she's harboring is unhealthy."

"Well, can you blame her? She believes they had something to do with her friend's death."

"True. I can relate to that. But I'm funneling all my

anger into this investigation. Maybe she'll find comfort in knowing that Todd and I are working overtime trying to solve the case."

"Speaking of Todd, is he coming tonight?"

"He's gonna try. He and a couple of other deputy sheriffs are meeting up to try and figure out who's behind all these attacks. So while he works that angle, I'll be working this one."

Rachel placed her empty glass on a server's tray and pick up a full one. "Way to tag-team. I like the two of you together."

"We do make a good team."

Rachel's right eyebrow arched. "I'm not talking professionally. I mean, don't get me wrong. You and Todd obviously work well together. I just think you'd play together even better."

"Mmm, maybe," Elle murmured coyly. "But first things first. Taylor's investigation supersedes all of that."

"Of course it does. But come on. You can't deny the connection between you and Todd."

Elle gazed at the champagne bubbles shooting through her glass. "There's definitely something brewing between us. We…uh…we actually kissed the other day."

"Oh, *did* you now? Exactly when did this happen? Where did this happen? And why are you just now telling me about it?"

"It happened the night Todd and I were at his house trimming the Christmas tree."

She deliberately withheld the information about their good-night kiss after the evening at Cozy's.

One kiss was enough info to share with her exuberant friend.

Rachel clapped her hands. "Eek!"

"Hold on. Don't get too excited. It wasn't that big of a deal. We'd probably just had too many glasses of wine…"

Elle's voice trailed off when she saw Sara shuffling toward them.

She was staring down at the white marble floor, clutching a beat-up brown tote bag. Her black-and-white houndstooth dress appeared two sizes too big, and her run-over loafers were riddled with scuff marks.

"Hey, Sara," Elle said. "Glad you could make it."

"I cannot believe you convinced me to come to this thing," Sara scoffed, her wide eyes darting around the room. "I feel so outta place. I don't belong here. Was that the *mayor* I saw on the way in? I think I should leave. *After* I get a drink."

"Sara," Elle said. "Relax. You're fine. You belong here just as much as anyone else."

"Absolutely," Rachel assured her. "It's nice to see you again. How've you been?"

The straps on Sara's tote slipped off her shoulder. The bag fell to the floor. She didn't bother to pick it up.

"*Terrible.* I'm exhausted. My boss made me work a double after three truckloads of pork came in unexpectedly. That's why I look a mess. I had to borrow this tent dress from my next-door neighbor because I didn't have anything to wear, and…" She spun around. "Where's the bar?"

Rachel pointed toward the back of the room. "In the corner. Right next to that statue of the man falling to his knees."

"Ew," Sara muttered. "He is creepy as hell. But not creepy enough to keep me away from the alcohol. You two good with your champagne or do you want something stronger?"

Elle nodded her head. "We're good. Thanks."

"Cool. Be right back."

The moment Sara walked off, Sloane came strolling toward the women.

"Hello, ladies," she purred, tossing her hair back and greeting them with air kisses.

"Hello, Sloane," Rachel said. "I'm so glad you could make it."

"Thank you. I'm excited to be here. I never would've missed a Pilar Samuels art opening. I am a huge fan. My husband and I actually own a few of her pieces."

Of course you do, Elle almost blurted out.

Sloane twirled around, and the hem of her red silk dress fluttered through the air. "The turnout is wonderful. Looks like all of Bradford's elite showed up. I saw several of the cultural center's board members when I walked in. And I had a lovely chat with the mayor before making my way back here."

"Oh, nice," Rachel replied, her squeaky voice reeking of insincerity.

Elle held her glass to her lips, hiding a snicker behind the rim.

"One person I was surprised to see," Sloane continued, "is *Sara*. How did she even know about this event?"

"I invited her," Rachel said. "I didn't want to leave her out considering she's one of our fellow Jewels."

Sloane shot her a look through the corners of her eyes, then turned up her nose.

"Well, I did make an oath to honor our sisterhood during the initiation process," Rachel added.

Sloane's matte red lips snarled in disgust. "Speaking of the devil. *Literally…*"

Sara came dancing toward them, her feet shuffling to the beat of the DJ's jazz record.

"Mmm!" she exclaimed. "This is the best rum and Coke I have ever had. Just between us, it's my second," she mumbled through the corner of her mouth. "I threw the first one back while I was chatting with the bartender. I coulda sworn I knew him from somewhere. BB's maybe?"

Sloane gritted her teeth as Sara slurped loudly from her glass.

"*Heeey*, Sloane," Sara sang. "What's going on, girl?"

"Good evening, Sara."

"Look, lady. It is so obvious that you can't stand me. Know how you can get rid of me for good?"

"No, but I'm sure you're going to tell me."

Sara took several steps toward Sloane, stopping inches away from her.

"Pay me back the money I—"

"Ladies," Rachel interrupted, attempting to slide in between them. "Please, let's all just calm down."

"Hello, everyone," Audrey said as she approached the group. "Is everything okay over here?"

Sloane and Sara were too busy staring each other down to respond.

"Not really," Elle whispered in Audrey's ear.

Rachel wrapped an arm around Sara and pulled her back. "Come on. This isn't the time or the place. Why don't you two table this discussion and revisit it at the next Precious Jewels meeting?"

"What did I miss?" Audrey asked Elle.

"A lot. We'll talk about it later."

Sloane ran her fingers through her hair and squared her shoulders. "You're right, Rachel. My apologies. This is a dignified, classy affair, and we should all act as such. Those of us who know how, at least."

"I should throw this drink in your face," Sara spewed.

"Looks to me like that glass is already empty," Sloane countered. She turned her back to Sara and faced Audrey. "Hello there. How are you? I haven't seen you since—well, you know."

"I'm hanging in there. Thank you for asking. How have you and the rest of The Precious Jewels been?"

"I'm doing well. We all are, for the most part. Aside from a few bad seeds sprinkled here and there." She cut her eyes at Sara before turning to address Audrey. "Listen, dear. I know you and I didn't end our relationship on the best of terms. But I hope we can make amends. Maybe you'll even consider rejoining The Precious—"

"Are you *serious*?" Sara interrupted. "Woman, you have no shame. Can't even lay off the recruiting for one night, you money-hungry hag."

"How *dare* you!"

Rachel nudged Elle as the women bickered back and forth. "Maybe putting these two in the same room together wasn't such a good idea."

"Maybe not. But let's stay tuned. Something interesting might come of it."

No sooner than the words were out of her mouth, Sara lunged toward Sloane.

"Look, *bitch*," she spat. "I did everything you asked me to do. *Everything*."

"What are you talking about? You're drunk."

"I'm not drunk. You know exactly what I'm talking about. And unless you want everybody in this room to know, too, you'd better gimme back my money!"

Sara poked Sloane in her bony chest. Sloane stumbled backward. Rachel grabbed her arm right before she crashed into a praying hands statue.

"Security!" Sloane screamed. "I've been assaulted! Security? Help!"

Rachel steadied Sloane while Elle held Sara back.

"Come on, Sloane," Rachel said. "You're okay. Why don't we step away for a minute? Go to my office and regroup."

Sloane stood straight up and smoothed her hair. "Fine. I'll follow you."

Sara lunged at her again when she walked by. Elle pulled Sara back right before her fist connected with Sloane's jaw.

"You'd better stop before Sloane calls the police on you," Elle warned.

"All right, all right. Fine. I'm good. You can let go of me now."

Elle waited until Sloane and Rachel were gone before releasing her.

Sara somehow managed to hold on to her drink. She drained the glass, then set it on a white marble pedestal.

"I need to get the hell outta here. That snitch probably is gonna call the cops on me. The last thing I need is another charge on my record."

Another charge?

Audrey, who'd managed to distance herself from the drama, threw Elle a knowing glance.

"It's been real, ladies," Sara said, throwing up a peace sign. "I'm gonna slip outta one of these side doors. Next time we meet up, it'll have to be at one of my spots. Deuces!"

Audrey waved feebly as Sara shuffled toward the back of the museum.

"See what I mean about her? That woman is trouble. Did you catch what she said about doing *everything* Sloane asked of her? What do you think she was talking about?"

"I have no idea. But I'm certainly going to find out."

"I bet you and *I* know what it's about. I'm telling you, Elle. Sloane had something to do with Taylor's murder. And she pulled Sara in to help her. She preyed on that poor woman. Now Sloane won't hold up her end of the bargain and pay Sara whatever she's owed. The whole situation is just shameful."

Elle's mouth went dry. "The thought of that even being a possibility makes me sick."

"Me, too! I think it's worth you and Todd looking into."

"So do I…"

Elle peered down the hallway, wishing she could hear what was going on in Rachel's office.

"And can you believe Sloane had the audacity to suggest I rejoin The Precious Jewels?" Audrey asked, her tone rising. "She must be out of her mind. This is too much. I *knew* I shouldn't have come here tonight."

"I'm glad you did. Because I never would've been able to recap all the drama we just witnessed."

Elle surveyed the room. Guests were busy chatting and studying the artwork. "I'm glad Sloane and Sara's altercation didn't disrupt the event. I guess we have the DJ to thank for that."

"True. He's kept the Christmas jazz going nonstop."

Elle's cell phone buzzed. A text message from Todd popped up.

Hey, the guys and I are still at it. Got an update. I reviewed the crime scene report taken after you were hit by the pickup at the forest preserve. Didn't realize there were photos of the truck's tire tracks. I emailed them to you for our personal file.

Excellent, Elle replied. Find anything else noteworthy?

Unfortunately, no. We combed the hiking trail again, where Taylor's and Harper's bodies were found. Got nothing. Now we're back at my house looking for shell casings or anything linked to the shooting. How are things going there?

Interestingly, to say the least. Sloane and Sara got into a huge argument. Sara said some incriminating stuff. Will share with you later. Guessing you won't be able to make it to the museum?

Doesn't look like it. Let me know when you're done. I'll give you a ride home and we'll catch up then.

"Hey," Audrey said, nodding toward the hallway. "Here come Sloane and Rachel. Looks like Sloane's pulled herself together."

The women approached.

Play your part. Show Sloane some support.

Elle placed a hand on her shoulder.

"Are you okay?"

"Yes. I'm fine. I just need to be kept away from that little degenerate." Sloane swiveled from side to side. "Where is she? Gone, I hope."

"She is."

"*Good.* Ladies? I'm going to brush that whole incident off as if it never happened. I'll also have mercy on she who shall go unnamed and won't press charges. Now, if you'll excuse me, I'm going to go over and say hello to Pilar."

Audrey grabbed Sloane's arm. "Wait, before you go, tell me. What was Sara talking about when she mentioned doing everything that you'd asked of her?"

Elle's eyes darted from Audrey to Sloane. She held her breath, anxious to hear her response.

"Oh, please. Don't listen to that delusional woman. She's just bitter. And intoxicated. Nothing was expected of her that wasn't asked of the other Jewels. Honor your commitment to the organization. Respect your fellow sisters. Make an effort to recruit new members…"

Audrey's head lowered as she ticked off the oaths.

"Sloane, you and I both know that Sara doesn't associate with women who can afford to join The Precious Jewels. That's why she feels so used. It's as if you stole her money and left her with nothing but false promises."

"You can thank your friend Taylor for that, may she rest in peace. Don't forget, she's the one who recruited Sara and made all of those false promises. Not me."

Linda, Sloane's right-hand woman, came rushing over.

"Sloane! Senator Butler just arrived. He's talking

to your husband and asked about you. You'd better get over there. *Stat!* Now would be the perfect time for you to discuss the idea of him planting a botanical garden on Jefferson Boulevard instead of building that wretched playground."

"Good idea. Ladies, if you'll excuse me."

Sloane and Linda bolted toward the front of the room. Elle turned to Rachel and Audrey, pressing her palm against her damp forehead. "What in the hell just happened?"

"Utter chaos," Rachel said, sighing heavily. "That's what happened. As much as I'd love to stand here and dissect that fiasco, I need to go and check on the guests."

Audrey embraced her. "I'm glad those two didn't ruin your event. Thank you again for inviting me. But I think I've had enough for tonight. I haven't been to a social outing in, gosh, I don't know how long. This one proved that I've been doing the right thing by staying home."

"Thank you again for coming. I wish it could've been under more pleasant circumstances, but…"

"No worries," Audrey said. "Maybe we can all get together for lunch sometime and make up for it. We'll talk soon."

Once Audrey was gone, Elle linked arms with Rachel. "And then there were two."

"Yeah, two who need something stronger than champagne after all that. Why don't we go grab another drink, then I'll introduce you to Pilar?"

"That sounds good. Can you give me a quick sec? I wanna send Sara a text. Make sure she's okay."

"How sweet." Rachel hesitated, peering at Elle

through squinted eyes. "Wait, why do I get the impression you're up to something more than just checking on her?"

"I'll meet you over by the bar and tell you all about it."

"Suit yourself, secret squirrel."

Elle pulled her cell from her overstuffed clutch and began composing a message.

Hey, just checking on you. Hope you're okay. Sorry things went left at the opening. Quick question, what were you referring to when you told Sloane you'd done everything she'd asked, yet she didn't uphold her end of the bargain? Just curious...

Elle sent the text, then headed toward the bar, hoping Sara would be sober enough to respond.

Chapter Sixteen

Todd pulled up in front of Elle's house.

"Thank you for the ride."

"You're welcome. Thanks for providing the entertainment the whole way here. I can't believe a Pilar Samuels art opening got that wild."

Elle pressed her hand against her forehead. "Neither can I. I'm just glad to be home."

"You know, I haven't seen your parents since you got to town. Are they here?"

"No, they're at the teachers' union's annual holiday party. They never miss it, even though my mother retired years ago."

"Aw, nice. Well, I'll try and catch them next time."

"You can still come in if you want."

Todd looked at the dashboard's clock. It was after 11:00 p.m.

"Are you sure it isn't too late?"

Elle threw her head back and laughed.

"What?" Todd asked, enamored by her bright smile. He fought the urge to lean over and kiss her.

"Sir, we are grown. Not only can I have company when my parents aren't home, but I can also do so whenever I want. Plus, you're not even considered company. You're family. Which means you're welcome anytime."

Just reach inside my chest and steal my heart, woman...

"That's a sweet thing to say," Todd murmured.

"It's the truth. I should also mention that my mother made a pot of her famous gumbo, which, if I recall correctly, you used to devour back in the day."

He turned off the engine. "Oh, you should've just led with that. Did she throw in everything that I love?"

"If you're referring to crab legs, chicken wings, shrimp, oysters and lobster, then yes. She did."

"Now I'm drooling. I'd love a bowl. Or three."

The pair climbed out of the car and headed toward the house.

"What if I told you she made hot water cornbread and peach cobbler, too?"

Todd pumped his fist in the air. "If you're trying to make me snatch your mother away from Mr. Scott so that *I* can marry her, it's working," he joked as Elle opened the front door.

"Please. There is nothing you could do to steal my mother from—"

She stopped midsentence. She stood in the doorway, staring into the dim living room.

"Todd. Something's wrong."

Elle ran her hand along the wall in search of the light switch. She took a step forward and stumbled over something. Todd quickly grabbed her.

"Are you okay?"

"I'll know as soon as I turn the light on," she breathed.

Elle flipped the switch then emitted a guttural scream. The living room had been ransacked. The couch and love seat were overturned. The midnight blue upholstery had been ripped apart.

Broken mosaic lamps were strewn across the hardwood floor, lying among shattered glass from the coffee and end tables.

"Oh my God," Elle sobbed into her hands. Tears rolled down her cheeks. She crept through the room, her legs shaking as she surveyed the damage.

Anger burned in the pit of Todd's stomach. He pulled out his cell phone and called Sheriff Glover. It went straight to voice mail.

"Sheriff, it's Jacobson. I need for you and the team to meet me at the Scotts' house as soon as possible. It's been vandalized."

He sent an emergency group text message to the sheriff's department, alerting them of the attack, then turned his attention back to Elle.

She was now frantically moving about, taking pictures of the damage with her cell phone.

"I am so sorry, Elle. The team will be here shortly. In the meantime, let's see what we can find without disturbing any possible evidence."

She approached him and collapsed. He caught her before she fell to the floor.

Elle's entire body trembled against his.

"I don't know how much more of this I can take, Todd. It's too much. Attacking me is one thing. But my *parents*?"

"I know, Elle. I know."

His cell phone rang.

"Hello?"

"It's Deputy Cross! Are you all okay?"

"Yes, we're fine. But you and the team need to get here immediately."

"We're already on the way. Just hang tight."

"Will do."

Elle clung to Todd tighter as he disconnected the call.

"Was that the sheriff's department?"

"It was. They're on the way. Once they get here, we'll examine the scene thoroughly and hopefully collect some evidence—"

"Wait!"

Elle pulled away from him and darted through the dining room.

Todd ran after her. "What's wrong?"

She was too busy hopping over the toppled oakwood chairs to respond.

He sped up, clipping his shin on the overturned dinner table's leg.

"Ouch! Elle, where are you going?"

"To my bedroom!"

Fragments of broken porcelain plates crunched underneath her pumps.

"Watch your step!" Todd insisted, grabbing her waist just as she slipped on a cream chair cover.

They ran up the stairs two at a time. Elle flung open her bedroom door. The room was in shambles.

The bed had been torn apart. Her silver comforter was balled up in one corner while the mattress lay in the other. The dresser drawers had been dumped and thrown about. Lamps were knocked to the floor. Makeup and toiletries were scattered everywhere.

Elle jetted toward her toppled desk and fell to her knees.

"Please be here." she panted. "*Please* be here…"

Todd bent down next to her. "What are you looking for?"

"My laptop. All the information we've collected for Taylor's case is on it. The police report, the research, our personal findings, theories…*everything*!"

Elle's breathing quickened as she ripped through the drawers.

"I'm about to have a panic attack. It's not here. It's not here!"

Todd placed his hands on her shoulders. "Elle, listen. Calm down. It's okay. I'm sure all the information was saved in the cloud. Plus, you've got a hard copy of the file, I've got everything saved on my computer—"

"That's not the point! Our attacker has the upper hand now. They know it all. Who our suspects are, what we're presenting to Sheriff Glover—"

Her voice broke. She fell back, slamming against her mirrored closet door.

Todd sat down and wrapped his arm around her. She leaned against his chest.

"Change in strategy, then," he said. "Let's meet with Sheriff Glover sooner than we'd planned. Since these attacks are only getting worse, law enforcement will have no choice but to step up and go all in on this investigation."

"Let's hope so. They should've done that a long time ago." Her head slumped. "After what happened tonight at the art opening, Sloane is looking more and more suspicious. To be honest, so is Sara. She really showed out. *Bad.* Her bitterness toward The Precious Jewels is something vicious. I think she'd do anything, and I do mean anything, to recoup that initiation fee."

"Didn't you say she left the event early tonight?" Todd asked.

Elle glanced around her ravaged bedroom, then slowly sat up. "Yes. She did."

Todd felt her body tense. She turned to him.

"Do you think Sara did this?"

"I think it's a strong possibility. If she did, let's just hope she left evidence behind to prove it."

Elle's cell phone buzzed.

"Oh, how convenient. This is Sara, finally replying to my text from earlier tonight."

"What'd she say?"

"She wrote, Hey Elle, sorry I'm just getting back to you. I went straight home after leaving the museum and passed out."

"Hmm. Already setting up her alibi possibly?"

"Could be. Then she wrote, To answer your question, I did something that I'm not proud of. Sloane offered me money to spy on the new group Taylor was putting together, and pass on whatever info I could. So I did. But Sloane never paid me. I'm still pissed about it."

"Damn," Todd muttered. "I feel so bad for my sister. Here she was, thinking Sara was her friend. And I know Taylor made some missteps. But that was just low-down. I hate that she was surrounded by so many awful people before she died."

Elle leaned her head against his shoulder. "Me, too. Taylor may have done some questionable things, but she didn't deserve this."

"How did Sara end the text?"

"By asking if I could keep everything she shared to myself."

"That's not gonna happen. I'll be passing that intel on to Sheriff Glover along with everything else we've collected."

Sirens blared in the distance.

"They're here!" Elle exclaimed.

The pair jumped up and jetted downstairs.

"I'd better call my parents and tell them what happened. I would hate for them to drive up and see all this without knowing."

"Good idea. In the meantime, I'll get together with the other officers and start collecting evidence. There's gotta be a fingerprint, droplets of blood from all this broken glass, *some* form of evidence that'll lead us to a suspect."

"Let's hope so this time."

Elle watched as Todd went to let his fellow officers inside.

Thank God I've got you here...

She walked back to the kitchen. It hadn't been touched. She turned on the light.

There, scrawled along the wall over the breakfast nook, was a message spray-painted in black.

Consider this your final warning. Leave Taylor's case alone and GET OUT OF BRADFORD!

Chapter Seventeen

The next evening, Todd and Elle sat across the street from The Ravenswood Lounge, which was a hot spot for Bradford's second-shift factory workers.

Sara was known to frequent the seedy bar often. Elle suggested to Todd that they fake an unexpected run-in and catch her off guard, hoping the mix of surprise and alcohol would lead to some answers.

"So it's official," Todd said. "Sara and Sloane are running neck and neck on your list of suspects."

"Yep. They sure are."

"If Sara is involved in Taylor's murder, I'll have to admit, she's pretty damn clever. Remember the way she interacted with us at BB's? Her behavior didn't exactly scream out suspect."

"She may just be a good actress. As well as an evil human being."

"As the famous poet Charles Baudelaire once said, the finest trick of the devil is to persuade you that he does not exist."

"Hmm, good one," Elle remarked. "With that being said, I still haven't ruled out our other suspects just yet. Along with Sloane and Sara, Chloe is still on my list. So is Bryce."

"Yeah, I haven't forgotten about that life insurance Bryce will be cashing out any day now."

"Neither have I. But do you know what I can't seem to shake?"

"What's that?"

"The comment Sloane made during The Precious Jewels meeting about wanting to strangle Sara. When I heard it, my mind immediately went to Taylor being choked to death."

"I thought you were going to say the break-in at your parents' house was what you couldn't shake. How'd they take it?" he asked.

"I think they were more worried about how I took it. They're staying with friends while the place is searched for evidence before the cleaning service comes in to get it back in order."

"And you?" he said, concern coloring his voice. "You feeling safe?" He'd dropped her at the local five-star hotel on that awful night after she talked to the officers in charge of the investigation.

"I am, thanks. I told my parents I'd go back home and check things out for them as soon as the house is in order again."

A run-down gray sedan pulled in front of the lounge.

Elle leaned into Todd and stared out of his window. "I think that's Sara's car."

"Are you sure?"

"Positive. I saw her driving it at Sloane's house."

Four men climbed out of the vehicle. No Sara.

"Doesn't look like she's with these guys," Todd said.

"No, she isn't. But the driver is her husband."

"Wait, which one was driving?"

"The big guy with the bald head and the scraggly beard."

"You know him?"

Elle pulled out her cell phone and opened Facebook. "Only through social media. Sara friended me last week. Her profile pic is a photo of them on their wedding day."

Todd eyed the phone screen. "Yep. That's definitely him. Gunnar Ross. Hmm, where do I know that name? Wait, didn't he go to Bradford High?"

"He did. He and Sara were a few years behind me."

Todd glanced out the window, studying Gunnar's bloodshot eyes and potbelly. "Yeah, it's coming back now. He was an all-star pitcher on the baseball team. There were write-ups on him in the local paper every week. He damn near made it to the majors. Until he got caught up in drugs."

"Wow. What a waste." Elle paused. "I wonder why Sara isn't with them tonight."

"You think she may have stayed late at the factory? Picked up an extra shift?"

"And missed out on a night of drinking with her buddies? I seriously doubt it. But hey, you never know. Maybe she's working extra hours to recoup the money she lost with Sloane and The Precious Jewels."

Todd's cell phone buzzed. He checked the message then grasped Elle's hand.

"Deputy Cross just got a call from the crime lab. Forensics lifted half of a bloody fingerprint from a porcelain plate at your parents' house."

"*Really?* That is awesome! At the rate we were going, I didn't think our suspect would ever screw up and leave any evidence behind."

"Hold on. Don't get too excited. They don't know

how good the quality of the print is just yet. Forensics is hoping they can lift it from the porcelain using the powder, brush and tape method."

"It'll work. It has to. And when it does, I pray the print matches a DNA profile in the FBI's database."

Todd watched the entrance to the lounge. Factory workers continued to pour inside. But still no Sara.

"What do you think?" he asked. "Should we just go in and grab a drink? Wait to see if she shows up later?"

"Might as well."

Todd stepped out of the car. He paused when Sara's husband and his friends came charging out of the bar.

"Wait, what's going on?"

"I have no idea." Elle walked around the car. "Is Gunnar crying?"

"Looks like it."

Gunnar jumped inside the car. His coworkers followed suit. He revved the engine, then sped off.

"Get back in the car," Todd said. "Let's follow them!"

His door was barely closed before Todd peeled away from the curb and flew to the corner. He slammed on the brakes. His head swiveled from right to left, then right again.

"Dammit! Did you see which way they went?"

"Left. Left!"

Todd turned onto Washington Boulevard and pressed down on the accelerator as they approached a yellow light.

"There they are!" Elle said, pointing toward Shoreham Street. "Make a right."

"I'm on it."

He turned the corner, careful to keep some distance between his car and theirs.

Todd peered into the car's back window. Everyone's heads were bobbing around frantically.

"Do you see them?" he asked. "They all look like they're freaking out about something."

"I wonder what's happening. Why'd they leave the bar so abruptly?"

"And where are they going?"

Gunnar blew through a red light and made a sharp right turn onto Piedmont Drive. Todd slowed down, making sure no cars were driving through the intersection before running the light and continuing after them.

Streams of smoke billowed from a tall, skinny chimney in the distance.

"Are they going to the factory?" Elle asked.

"That's what it looks like. But why would they be going back to work? Didn't they just leave from there?"

"That's what I thought."

Todd steered the car along the winding, narrow road. Ackman's Meat Packing Plant appeared up ahead.

Gunnar swerved into the massive parking lot. He slammed on the brakes right in front of the dingy gray building.

The group climbed out and ran toward the entrance.

A security guard stopped them before they went inside.

"What in the hell is going on?" Todd asked before pulling into a nearby space.

"I don't know. But we're about to find out."

Todd pulled her back. "Wait. Don't get out just yet. I don't want Gunnar to see us and realize we were following him. Let's hang back and see what happens."

He rolled down the windows, listening in as Gunnar pointed a finger in the guard's face.

"Where is my wife?" he yelled. "I wanna see my wife!"

The guard gripped Gunnar's shoulder. "Just hold on, sir. The ambulance is on the way."

"Ambulance," Elle said. "Todd, I think you should—"

His cell phone buzzed just as sirens rang out.

"Deputy Cross is calling me."

"Good. Maybe he knows what's going on."

He picked up the call. "What's up, Cross?"

"Jacobson, I know you're off the clock. But I wanted to let you know that a woman's been attacked over at the meat processing plant."

Todd put the call on speaker. "Do you know the name of the victim?"

"Yes. Sara Ross."

"What?" Elle gasped, gripping the door handle. "What happened?"

"Is she alive?" Todd asked.

"Barely. I don't have all the details just yet. But from what I've gathered, she's in critical condition. I'll know more once I get down there."

"My God," Elle whispered, covered her mouth. "I cannot believe this…"

"I'm actually at the plant now," Todd told Deputy Cross. "The victim must still be inside."

An ambulance sped through the lot and drove around to the back of the factory. Several squad cars followed.

"No," Deputy Cross said. "She was found outside. Around back, in the employee parking lot. It's been reported that she was taking a smoke break. My guess is that someone snuck up on her. Caught her completely off guard."

"Let's get back there," Elle whispered. "Now!"

"All right, Cross. I'll see you when you get here."

"Ten-four."

Todd disconnected the call and turned to Elle. She stared straight ahead, her eyes filling with tears.

"Are you okay?"

"Not really. I—I am in complete shock. I guess we can cross Sara off our list of suspects."

"And then there were two."

"Three," Elle rebutted. "Don't forget Chloe." She slouched down in her seat and jammed her hands underneath her arms. "This case is getting so twisted that I can barely keep up anymore."

Todd drove around to the back of the factory. Security had blocked off the entrance to the lot. He flashed his badge and was let through.

The scene was chaotic. Frenzied factory workers crowded the sidewalk, craning their necks to see what was happening. Law enforcement struggled to keep them at bay.

Deputies swarmed the parking lot. Paramedics were standing over Sara's body, transporting her onto a stretcher.

Todd crept past the scene. Sara's eyes were shut, and a brace had been secured around her neck.

"Oh no," Elle whimpered. "It looks like she's gone!"

"Stay calm. Sara is not dead. If she were, they wouldn't be giving her oxygen."

Elle patted her heaving chest. "You're right. I just wonder how she managed to stay alive. Our suspect's modus operandi seems to be death. Every time."

"My guess is that one of her coworkers entered the lot before the suspect could finish the job."

Sheriff Glover spoke with paramedics as they placed Sara inside the ambulance.

"Just get her to the hospital!" he yelled, frantically waving his hands. "Do everything in your power to keep that woman alive!"

Todd parked near the back of the lot. "I have never seen the sheriff lose his cool. Maybe he's finally realizing that there's more to this situation than he'd originally thought."

"Good. Hopefully that'll motivate him to reexamine Taylor's and Harper's deaths. He's gotta know that they're all connected."

"Listen," Todd said before stepping out of the car, "you're gonna have to lay low and stay here while I find out what's happening."

"I can do that. Hey, is it okay if I call Rachel and update her on all this?"

"Yeah, just make sure she keeps it to herself. I don't see any media here, so I'm guessing word hasn't gotten out yet. I'd like to keep it that way until Sheriff Glover is ready to release the information to the public."

"I will. We can trust Rachel."

"I'll be back soon."

"Take notes!"

Todd gave her a thumbs-up and headed toward the scene.

Elle's fingers trembled as she dialed Rachel's number. Her friend picked up on the first ring.

"Hey!" Rachel panted, sounding out of breath. "I was literally just dialing your number."

"You were? Why?"

"You haven't heard the news? Sara was attacked down at the factory."

"I did hear the news. That's why I was calling you. I'm actually at the factory right now with Todd. But wait, how did you find out?"

"My cousin Al is their quality control manager. He called and told me. Do you know whether or not Sara's still alive?"

"She is. But she's in critical condition. The ambulance is taking her to the hospital now."

"Oh my God," Rachel moaned. "I pray that she'll be okay. What in the world is happening to our town?"

Elle's entire body went numb as she watched paramedics work on Sara. "Somebody is wreaking havoc all over Bradford. That's what's happening."

"Have you talked to Audrey?"

"No. Why? Have you?"

"I ran into her at the grocery store last night. She said that Sara came storming into the car dealership yesterday afternoon, demanding to see Bryce. When he came out of his office, she confronted him about the money she paid to join The Precious Jewels."

"Why would she do that?" Elle asked.

"According to Sara, she thinks Bryce should reimburse her initiation fee since Taylor's the one who convinced her to join the group, and she's no longer here to do it."

"What? You have got to be kidding me."

"Unfortunately, I'm not."

"It sounds like she was really starting to unravel. I wonder what prompted her to barge into the dealership and confront Bryce like that."

"It could be the fact that her husband found out about that second mortgage she took out on their house," Rachel said.

Elle shot straight up in her seat. "Oh no. Did he?"

"He sure did. And he told Sara that if she didn't get their money back ASAP, he would divorce her. Audrey said things got so heated at the dealership between Sara and Bryce that he had to call security and have her escorted off the property."

"So Sara pops up unexpectedly at Bryce's job yesterday and confronts him over the whole Precious Jewels debacle. Then today, someone attempts to murder her."

"Yep," Rachel chirped. "That's it in a nutshell."

Elle watched as Todd and the other officers huddled in a circle, having what looked to be an intense conversation. A few deputies were busy interviewing some of the workers. A forensic investigator was picking up items off the ground and placing them in plastic bags.

"It is taking everything in me not to get out of the car and go share this with Todd. But I'm not supposed to be here, so I'll wait." She bit down on her thumbnail. "Bryce just got bumped up to the *top* of my suspects list."

"Rightfully so."

"I think it's time for Todd and me to pay him another visit. Oh, speaking of Todd," Elle said as he headed toward the car, "here he comes. I'll brief him on everything, then figure out what's next. Thanks for the info."

"Anytime. Keep me posted."

Todd's expression was grim when he climbed inside the car.

"Any word on Sara's condition?"

"She's alive. Unconscious, but alive. The bruises around her neck are an indication that she was strangled. Paramedics don't know how long she may have gone without oxygen. So the doctors will run tests and see if there's any brain activity."

Elle pressed her hands against the sides of her face, struggling not to choke up.

Deep breath. Suck it up. Now is not the time for tears. You've got a case to solve.

"We need to go to Bryce's house," she said. "I'll explain why on the way there."

"Right now?"

"Yes. *Right* now."

Chapter Eighteen

Todd turned down Bryce's block. As they drove toward his house, Elle noticed that the front door was open.

Bryce stepped outside. Someone hovered behind him in the doorway.

"Looks like Bryce has company," Elle said. "I wonder who that is."

Todd slowed down. "I can't tell from here. But we're about to find out."

"Let's do so discreetly. Don't let him see us."

Todd pulled over near the curb on the opposite side of the street, creeping slowly toward the house.

Whoever was standing in Bryce's doorway wrapped their arms around him.

"What in the world is he doing?" Elle asked.

"Looks to me like he's hugged up on some woman." Todd's acidic tone was filled with venom. "My loathing for that man just keeps on growing. Right along with all the reasons he wanted Taylor dead."

Elle's stomach churned in disgust. "Taylor hasn't been buried a good two months and he's already out here dating. What happened to the mourning? And the tears? And the claims that he misses his wife so much?"

"I know, right? He was just putting on a show for us."

Bryce stepped to the side. Opened the door wider. A red high heel attached to a long leg hit the porch.

"Wait, here she comes," Elle whispered, as if someone might hear her.

She and Todd peered through the windshield.

The woman stepped outside.

It was Audrey.

What the...

Elle emitted an audible gasp. Her limbs shook with fury. She grabbed the door handle.

Todd pulled her back.

"Don't," he warned. "Be cool. Let's just wait and see how this is gonna play out."

As soon as the words were out of his mouth, Audrey pressed her body against Bryce's. He wrapped his arms around her waist. The pair indulged in a long, deep, passionate kiss.

"I think I'm gonna be sick," Elle choked.

Several moments passed before the pair finally pulled away from each other. They glanced up and down the street before sharing one last kiss. She then hurried toward her car, which was parked several houses down from his.

"Oh, please!" Elle said. "If your plan was to be discreet, you failed. *Miserably.*"

Todd hit the accelerator and made a U-turn, parking right in front of Bryce's house.

"Time to go and get a confession."

BRYCE SAT ON the edge of the couch, staring down at the floor. Elle was seated next to him, and Todd was on the adjacent love seat.

They had him boxed.

"I cannot believe what I just saw," Elle said. "You know, we were originally coming here to ask about your confrontation with Sara Ross at the dealership yesterday."

Bryce remained silent.

Elle studied his body language. Looked for a sign of guilt. Fidgeting. Twitching. Shifting in his seat. *Anything.*

Bryce was perfectly still.

"Why didn't you call the sheriff's department and report the incident with Sara?" Todd asked. "Better yet, why didn't you call us while she was there so that we could pick her up for disturbing the peace?"

"Come on, man," Bryce said, waving Todd off. "I wasn't worried about that silly woman and her ridiculous claims. That situation was between her and Taylor. It had nothing to do with me. I didn't even want to waste the authorities' time on it. So I handled the matter myself."

Elle and Todd exchanged curious glances.

"What do you mean, you handled the matter yourself?" she asked.

"I called security and had her removed from the premises."

"Did you do anything else to *handle it*?" Todd probed.

Bryce finally looked up, staring Todd directly in the eye. "What do you mean?"

"Exactly what I asked."

Bryce hesitated. "Um…no. All I did was call security. They came right away and escorted Sara off the property. She complied, *reluctantly*, but she complied. Nothing else needed to be done."

Todd nodded his head discreetly at Elle. It was her cue to let it go.

"Listen," Bryce said. "There's something I haven't told you all."

"Humph," Elle uttered under her breath. "Ya think?"

"And what would that be?" Todd asked.

"This...this is tough to talk about—" Bryce sputtered before his voice broke.

"Look, whatever is going on here," Todd said, "it's time for you to get it off your chest. I know this entire situation has been weighing heavily on you. Just release it. Free yourself from the burden of your secrets and admit the truth."

Bryce extended his legs and bent over, as if trying to catch his breath. His brown skin had turned a pale shade of gray. His cheeks were smeared with tears.

The look of a guilty man...

"Taylor knew that she was going to die," he blurted out.

Elle and Todd stared at each other blankly, both completely dumbfounded.

"Excuse me?" Elle asked. "How did she know that?"

He just sat there, quietly weeping.

"Bryce," Todd said firmly, "what do you mean? How did Taylor know that?"

"A couple of weeks before her death, Taylor told me that she was having dreams and visions of someone wanting to kill her."

"Someone?" Todd asked. "Who exactly was it?"

"I don't know. I got the feeling that *she* knew. But when I asked, she wouldn't say."

Elle thought about Taylor's journal entry in her Precious Jewels notebook. "Did she ever mention being followed, or harassed?"

Bryce's eyes closed as he pressed his fingertips into his forehead. "Not that I can recall."

"Do you remember her saying anything about receiving threats?"

"No. *Wait*...no. Only in the visions. Or the dreams, or...whatever the hell they were. All this chaos has me confused."

Bryce slammed his hand against the arm of the couch.

Elle jolted forward, startled by the gesture. She wondered if it was a sign of pain. Or guilt. Or both.

Either way, she and Todd were determined to keep going until they got some answers.

"Did my sister know that you were cheating on her, Bryce?"

Silence.

Elle tightened her jaws, willing herself not to reach over and slap Bryce across the face. Regardless of their financial woes, his infidelity was inexcusable.

Bryce turned on the waterworks again.

"No," he sobbed. "She didn't."

Elle dug her fingernails into her thighs as her frustration grew. If Bryce's tears were a call for sympathy, he wouldn't be getting any.

"How long has this affair between you and Audrey been going on?" she asked.

He shrugged. "A few months or so. Maybe four or five. I don't know."

"Of all the women you could've cheated with, why would you choose one of Taylor's friends?"

"No. That is not how it happened. Audrey and I

were already involved before she and Taylor became friends."

"Oh, okay, cool," Todd interjected smugly. "That makes it all right, then."

Bryce ignored the comment. "Taylor practically forced herself on Audrey, pressuring her to hang out and whatnot. And it was all so superficial. Taylor just wanted to recruit Audrey into that—that Positive Gems group or whatever."

Elle didn't have the energy to correct him. Instead she pressed on toward getting a confession.

"Audrey seems to think that she and Taylor shared a genuine friendship. Aside from the fact that she was sleeping with her husband, of course. But I digress."

Bryce held his hands in the air and opened his mouth.

Elle kept going, uninterested in hearing his defense.

"So did you and Audrey meet when she started working at the car dealership?"

"No. We, uh, we met before that. At a car show. *Damn*, this is embarrassing," he whimpered before burying his face in his hands.

"Well, the cat's out of the bag now," Todd said. "So you may as well keep going."

"I'm so sorry, you guys—"

Todd leaped from the love seat so abruptly that Elle thought he might pounce on Bryce. But instead he began pacing the floor. "Look, save the apology. Just tell me what the hell was going on between you and my sister before you killed her!"

Bryce hopped up and marched toward Todd. "What did you just say to me?"

Todd placed his hand behind his back.

Elle knew what was there, propped inside his waist-band. His gun.

"You heard me," Todd said. "But I'll repeat myself since you wanna play dumb. What was going on be-tween you and Taylor before you—"

Bryce lunged at him before he could finish.

Elle quickly swooped in, wedging herself between the two men just as they made contact.

"Hey!" she yelled. "Stop it. Relax. Both of you!"

They leaned into her, neither wanting to back down. Her hands were pressed against their chests. Both of their hearts pounded erratically.

"Todd, Bryce, please. Let's sit back down and talk this out like adults."

Bryce reached over Elle's head and pointed his fin-ger in Todd's face. "That's what I was trying to do until he accused me of murder!"

Elle heard the click of Todd's gun being cocked. He pushed Bryce's hand away.

"If you ever stick your finger in my face like that again," Todd spat, "I swear I'll kill you."

"Go ahead, man. Do it!"

Elle pushed them both away and pulled out her cell phone. "How about I call Sheriff Glover and let him settle this situation for us. Huh? How does that sound?"

"Sounds good to me," Bryce said. "That way I can file a report stating that Deputy Sheriff Todd Jacobson just threatened my life—"

"And I can write you up for assaulting an officer!"

Todd's cell phone rang.

"Saved by the bell, *bitch*," he muttered.

"Man, you'd better—"

"Bryce!" Elle interrupted, pulling him toward the couch. "Come on. Let it go. Have a seat."

"Deputy Jacobson," Todd barked into the phone. "Wait, slow down, Cross. I can't understand you. What happened?"

Bryce took a seat. "I'm cool," he told Elle. "I'm actually glad everything's out in the open now. I feel like a weight's been lifted off me."

"This is not good," Todd grumbled. "At all…"

Elle spun around. "What's wrong?"

He looked up at her, his face twisted with frustration. "Sara is dead."

Chapter Nineteen

Sloane stood at the podium in front of her great room, banging the gavel down hard on the block.

"Ladies! May I have your attention, please? I would like to call this emergency meeting to order."

The room continued to buzz with frantic chatter.

"Ladies!" she screamed. "I would like to call the meeting to order. Now!"

An abrupt silence filled the air. All eyes turned to Sloane, who was visibly shaking.

Elle hadn't recognized her when she arrived at the meeting. Gone was Sloane's sleek hair, overdone makeup and perfectly tailored suit. Her hair was pulled back into a severe bun. Her face appeared pale, almost sickly, without the filled-in eyebrows, false eyelashes and overlined lips. A black velour leisure suit had replaced the Chanel blazer and skirt. Satin slippers covered her feet rather than designer stilettos.

Rachel tilted her head toward Elle. "Looks like somebody is crumbing underneath the weight of their actions."

"Thank you all for coming on such short notice," Sloane said. "I do wish that we were here under more pleasant circumstances. But unfortunately, we're not.

As you all know by now, we lost one of our fellow Precious Jewels. Our sister Sara Ross."

Whispers swept through the room. Sloane held up her hands.

"Please, everyone. Let me finish. I will allow questions once I'm done. But for the time being, I've got the floor. Now, I'll be the first one to admit that Sara and I did not have the best relationship. We certainly weren't on good terms when her life was cut short. But I've heard the rumors. And frankly, I am…"

Her voice cracked. She pressed her unmanicured hand against her chest.

"I am appalled. I would have never harmed that woman. Let alone *killed* her."

"That woman," someone mocked from the back of the room. "But didn't you threaten to strangle *that woman* at our last meeting?"

"Exactly," another member chimed in. "And what about that fight you two had at the art museum? Did you really slap Sara and have her arrested?"

Sloane picked up the gavel and slammed it down so hard that it broke.

An audible gasp swept across the room.

She stood at the podium, her back erect as she trembled from head to toe. "How sad is it that you people don't know me better than this. My character. My servitude. Look at all that I've done for this town. For all of *you*! I made you somebody. I lined those designer pocketbooks of yours with thousands of dollars."

"Not all of us!" someone shouted.

"Shut up!" Sloane screamed so violently that she stumbled backward.

Linda ran over and helped steady her.

"Get away from me!" Sloane insisted, pushing Linda so roughly that she almost fell into the Christmas tree. "I'm fine."

Rachel nudged Elle's arm. "Oh my word. That lady is far from fine."

"She is completely unraveling, right before our very eyes."

Sloane grabbed her highball glass and took a long sip of Scotch and soda. It was a far cry from her normal meeting drink of choice—a mimosa.

"Please excuse my outburst," she sniffed. "I am in mourning, as are all of you. It isn't easy losing two women you consider sisters, despite being on rocky terms."

"Three," Elle muttered. "Let's not forget Harper Mitchell."

Sloane clapped her hands. "Quiet!" she hollered in Elle and Rachel's direction. "Now, as I was saying, I have heard the rumors. And I am taking this moment to tell all of you that I had nothing to do with Taylor and Sara's deaths. *Nothing*."

She pointed over at Linda, who was standing nearby but keeping a safe distance.

"We would now like to open up the floor for questions," Linda said. "But before we do so, please, ladies, be respectful. Also, note that after today, Sloane does not plan on addressing this unfortunate situation again."

Rachel held her hand to her mouth. "That is until she gets called down to the station for questioning."

"Elle? Rachel?" Linda called out. "Do either of you have questions?"

"No, ma'am," Rachel replied. "I was just telling Elle that I need to get back to the museum soon."

Emma Green, a newer member of The Precious Jewels, stood up. "I have a question. Sloane, why wouldn't you just give Sara her initiation fee back and let her out of the organization? That wasn't very sisterly of you. Maybe she'd still be alive if you weren't being so selfish and greedy, and—"

"*Excuse* me," Linda interrupted. "Did you not hear the part where I asked for everyone to be respectful?"

"Do you hear how she is speaking to me?" Sloane asked Linda. "The anger in her tone? And the hostility?"

Linda patted her on the arm. "Yes, I know. You're right. It sounded awful…"

Chatter among the group picked up.

Sloane pointed at various women sitting around the room. "And do you notice a pattern here, Linda? All of these members who are disrespecting me are Taylor's recruits. They have truly brought down the integrity of my organization. Maybe one of *them* had something to do with the deaths—"

"Does anyone else have a question?" Linda asked, quickly interrupting Sloane.

Rachel nudged Elle. "You should ask Sloane where you can find your laptop."

"Better yet, why don't we sneak off and do a search of the house? I'm sure it's around here somewhere."

Several women stood and began talking at once.

"Uh-oh," Elle uttered. "This meeting is about to turn into a riot. Sloane should have hired a security company to keep things in order. Because she and Linda alone aren't cutting it."

Sloane picked up her glass and threw it across the room. It shattered against the gold frame of an oceanic oil painting.

All eyes turned to her.

"Meeting adjourned," she said before fleeing the room.

Half of the members chased after her while the other half tried to hold them back.

"Welp, it looks like Sloane has completely shut down," Rachel said. "I don't think anything else is going to come of this meeting. Should we leave?"

A shoe went flying through the air.

"Yes!" Elle declared. "Let's get the hell out of here."

The women hurried past the chaos and slipped out of the house.

"Whew!" Elle sighed. "That was a lot."

"Too much. Should we unpack it all over eggnog cocktails at Cozy's?"

"Most definitely."

They climbed inside of Rachel's white two-seater and headed to the restaurant.

"At this point," Rachel said, "Sheriff Glover has got to realize that all of these murders are linked. Haven't you and Todd gathered enough evidence to convince him that Sloane needs to be investigated?"

"Yes. We have. But it's all circumstantial. Todd wants to wait until we've gathered solid, direct evidence that supports our claim before we present anything to the sheriff." She also knew the sheriff had rebuffed Todd before, so he was determined to be extra sure before going to him again.

"Plenty of people have been convicted based on circumstantial evidence."

Elle's lips twisted with doubt. "Not when you're Sloane Whitlock, also known as the queen of Bradford."

"What about the bloody fingerprint that was found

at your parents' house? Have the results come back on it?"

"Yep. And it didn't match up with anyone's in CODIS."

"Wow. So you mean to tell me that this maniac, who's committing all these heinous crimes, has managed to stay out of the system?" Rachel asked.

"That's exactly what I'm telling you."

"We are dealing with a certified psychopath here."

Rachel made a right turn down Steward Avenue. A silver Range Rover pulled in front of them. "Hey, is that Chloe?"

Elle craned her neck, squinting through the windshield. "I don't think so. Looks like an older woman. But speaking of Chloe, I'm surprised that she wasn't at the meeting."

"Me, too. I texted her yesterday to find out if she'd heard about Sara, but she never responded. I didn't make a big deal out of it since I thought I'd see her today."

"That's strange. She stays on top of her phone and usually responds to texts within minutes."

Rachel tapped her palm against the steering wheel. "She never misses a Precious Jewels meeting, either. I hope she's okay."

"I have a feeling that Chloe is perfectly fine. Might just be keeping a low profile."

"Hmm, interesting. Wait, I see where you're going with this. And if that's the case, then you and Todd need to keep her close on your radar."

"We definitely haven't ruled her out." Elle rolled down her window, letting the crisp afternoon air cool her overheating skin. "Chloe still has a permanent spot on my list of suspects."

Rachel turned into Cozy's parking lot. Christmas music piped through the outdoor speakers. A four-foot-tall mechanical Santa Claus waved at customers as they entered the restaurant. A server stood near the doorway, passing out dessert samples.

"I can't remember the last time I was in Bradford during the holidays," Elle said. "I really wish I could enjoy all the festivities this year."

"You'll get to enjoy them again. You and Todd are on the cusp of solving this case. Where do you think you'll go from here?"

Elle paused as she fidgeted with her pearl drop earring. "I think it's time for us to take a deeper dive. Maybe pay Harper Mitchell's husband a visit. See what he might know."

Chapter Twenty

Todd let up on the accelerator as he crossed into Madison, which was two towns over from Bradford.

"How long has it been since you've visited this place?" he asked Elle.

"It's been years. And from the looks of it, the town is nothing like it used to be."

The main thoroughfare, once lined with quaint mom-and-pop shops, now housed a slew of chain restaurants, clothing stores and hotels.

"Yeah, a lot's changed," Todd said. "The town's population has doubled over the past few years. You should see it during the summer. Tourists everywhere."

"I guess that explains all new lodging along Hartford Boulevard."

Todd tapped the navigation screen. "It's also what brought Harper's husband back to North Carolina from Florida. I heard he's the primary builder behind most of this new construction. He's putting up a multiplex entertainment center at the site where we're meeting him. It's gonna be huge. Movie theaters, a beer garden, live concert venue. The works."

"I'm actually surprised he agreed to talk with us considering his tumultuous history with Harper."

"Well, he was never named a suspect in her death. Plus he doesn't know what we know. As far as he's concerned, we aren't aware of their pending divorce and his criminal record."

"Never even named a suspect," Elle muttered, "despite violating Harper's order of protection and trying to strangle her. That's a damn shame."

Todd stopped at a red light, watching as a group of high schoolers dressed in elf costumes crossed the street. "It'll be challenging not to bring any of that up. I'm not promising that I won't, either."

"Neither am I," she said. "But I think we should focus on what Keaton knows about Harper's involvement with The Precious Jewels."

"Agreed. If it does creep into the conversation, however, I'll make an effort to at least be decent."

"In one thousand feet," the voice navigation announced, "make a left turn. Your destination will be on the right."

"Have you gotten any updates on Sara's investigation?" Elle asked.

"Last I heard, Sheriff Glover was looking into one of her coworkers. Apparently, Sara was in the middle of a battle with a fellow lineman who'd suffered a shoulder injury. He didn't want to take an unpaid leave and heal up properly, so he kept coming to work but wasn't pulling his weight on the assembly line."

Elle held up her hand. "So wait, the sheriff's department is trying to pin this on a coworker?"

"That's what it's looking like. Sara and this team assembler got into a huge altercation the day she was attacked. And it just so happens that he was unaccounted for during the time of the assault."

"Was he able to explain his whereabouts?"

"He claimed that he'd left the floor and gone to cool off in one of the meat freezers. The deputies are looking through surveillance footage to see if it'll back his statement. This isn't the first time he and Sara have had an altercation, either. They got into a minor scuffle earlier this year over a similar issue. Sara ended up getting hit with a simple assault charge."

Elle thought back on the event at the art museum. "So that's the charge Sara was referring to the night she fought with Sloane. *Whew*. And the plot continues to thicken."

Todd turned down Cobb Court. The framework of a massive structure appeared up ahead.

Grassy knolls were filled with piles of dirt, wood and steel beams. The street was packed with dozens of bulldozers. A sea of construction workers milled about, hauling materials and reviewing sets of drawings.

"How in the world are we supposed to find Keaton in all this chaos?" Elle asked.

"I told him I'd send a text when we got here. I'm not gonna even attempt to drive any farther down this road."

Just as Todd began composing the message, there was a knock at the window. He and Elle jumped in their seats.

"Sorry, didn't mean to startle you!"

Todd rolled down the window. "No worries. You must be Keaton."

"I am. Deputy Jacobson?"

"Yes, and this is Elle Scott."

"Good to meet you both. Why don't you leave your

car here? We'll walk over to our makeshift coffee shop and talk there."

"You bet."

As Todd pulled closer to the curb, he noticed how different Keaton looked from the photo posted on his company website. With his scruffy beard and dark, shoulder-length hair, he appeared more like a rugged cowboy than a business owner.

His blue eyes were dull, and his bowlegged gait was slow. While still handsome, Keaton appeared weighed down. Grief-stricken, even.

"I'm a little surprised by this guy," Todd said when he and Elle stepped out of the car. "He seems pretty pleasant. Sad, but pleasant."

"Yeah, well, people who've encountered Jeffrey Dahmer have said that he was pleasant, too. Yet he killed and ate people. So keep your guard up."

"Touché."

Keaton approached with hard hats in hand. "Safety first."

He led them to a white, heated tent. Evergreen garland hung from its sloped roof. Folding tables and chairs were set up near the back. A barista wearing a Santa hat and snowman apron stood behind the wooden counter, passing out hot drinks and doughnuts.

"As you can see, I'm trying to keep things festive around here," Keaton said. "I really appreciate how hard my guys are working to complete this project. During the holiday season, no less."

Todd studied the development's intricately designed, multilevel buildout. "Looks like it's gonna be a spectacular complex."

"That's the plan." Keaton paused. "Building this

entertainment center was actually Harper's idea. I just wish she were here to see it." He pulled a handkerchief from his jeans back pocket and ran it across his face. "Why don't we grab a coffee and have a seat?"

Todd tapped Elle's hip. She nodded discreetly. They were both on the same page—surprised by the way Keaton spoke of his estranged dead wife.

The barista had already poured three drinks for the group by the time they reached the counter.

"Thanks, Lisa," Keaton said. He handed Todd and Elle their cups, then led them to a table near the back of the tent.

"We really appreciate you meeting with us," Elle said.

"I'm happy to do so. Bradford PD really dropped the ball on my wife's case. Her death was no accident, and no one can tell me otherwise. As far as I'm concerned, it's a cold case. So, nice to know someone cares enough to look into it a year later."

"What do you think happened to Harper?" Todd asked.

"Honestly? I think someone in that women's group she'd joined killed her."

"Are you referring to The Precious Jewels?"

"Yes. That…that cult."

"Why do you think they were involved?"

Keaton pushed his coffee cup to the side and folded his hands. "Harper and I had a great marriage before she joined that group. But then, once she became a member, everything changed. She was brainwashed into thinking they were all about sisterhood, and charity, and prosperity. In reality, those women are a bunch of scam artists. Harper paid out a huge sum of money to become a part of their scheme."

"From what I've heard," Todd said, "a lot of the members' husbands have a problem with the money their wives pour into the group. Did you?"

"Of course not. Look around you. I'm rich. Why would I care about that? My problem was that The Precious Jewels became an obsession for Harper. She loved competition, which turned into an addiction. The woman who ran that group touted it as a family. But she pitted the members against one another. It was all about who could bring in the most recruits. Level up the fastest. Gain the most status among Bradford's elite. Just ridiculous."

Todd took a swig of his coffee. He watched Keaton over the rim of the cup, expecting his expression to appear distorted with anger. But it was neutral. His eyes, however, drooped with sadness.

Keaton had caught Todd off guard. The man was actually making sense. Even more surprising was the fact that Todd felt sorry for him.

"What's the name of that group's ringleader again?" Keaton asked.

"Sloane Whitlock."

He snorted loudly. "Yes. Sloane Whitlock. *Man*, that woman is evil."

"Why do you think that?" Elle asked.

Todd almost chuckled at the airy innocence in her tone.

"Sloane has bad intentions. She's all about money, power and prestige. That woman is willing to do whatever it takes to attain all three. Like I said, she's running a cult. She uses her charm to possess those women, to the point where she can control them. Once she gains that control? They start to worship her."

"And you believe that Harper fell victim to Sloane's beguiling ways?"

"Absolutely. Full disclosure? I lost my wife to The Precious Jewels way before she died. Back then I was in Florida a lot for work. Harper chose to spend more time here with them rather than there with me."

Todd was tempted to interrupt him and address Harper's abuse allegations. But he bit his tongue and let Keaton finish.

"And I'm not proud to admit this, but at one point, I started seeing other women. I was chasing after what was missing in my marriage. Harper eventually found out. Rather than leave The Precious Jewels behind and work on our relationship, she filed for divorce."

Now's the time. Ask about the restraining order...

"Have you heard about the other deaths that are linked to The Precious Jewels?" Elle interjected before Todd could speak up.

"I have. I told Todd how sorry I am to hear of Taylor's passing. Just like Harper, I understand that law enforcement ruled her death as accidental. But a lot of people suspected her husband had something to do with it. Isn't that usually the case, though? The husband's always guilty, right?"

Todd shrugged, tilting his head back and forth. "Well, in many cases, yes. He is."

"It wasn't in mine," Keaton shot back, snatching off his hard hat and slamming it onto the table.

Todd winced at the loud thud.

"I don't think that was the case in Taylor's death,

either," Keaton continued. "If you wanna find Harper and Taylor's killer, take a closer look at that cult."

Elle turned to Keaton and gently placed her hand on his arm. "Let me ask you a question. Don't you find it odd that there are now three women linked to The Precious Jewels who were murdered, and they were all having trouble in their marriages?"

"Wait, what do you mean *three*? I thought the woman who was attacked at the factory survived."

"She did initially. But she didn't make it."

"Damn," Keaton mumbled, balling up a napkin and tossing it across the table.

"You know," Todd said, "you seem like a decent guy. But Elle and I have heard some things about your marriage that are pretty alarming."

"Oh, really? Like what? The restraining order she took out on me? And how I allegedly violated it?"

"Allegedly?" Elle chimed in. "The record shows that you did violate it. By strangling Harper, no less."

Keaton sat back and tucked his hands underneath his arms. When he began snickering, Todd almost reached over and snatched him up by the collar.

"Oh, is that funny?"

"Actually, yes. It is."

Todd and Elle both sat in silence, stunned by Keaton's response.

"Let me explain. When Harper left Florida and went back to Bradford, she took a very expensive antique scarf that belonged to my mother. My mom had passed away a few months prior. That scarf meant the world to me. Harper knew that. So I flew to Bradford to get it back."

"But Harper's neighbor reported that she saw you strangle her," Todd said.

"I did not strangle her. I'd asked her to please leave the scarf in the doorway. My plan was to get it, then go on about my business. Harper decided to come outside with the scarf wrapped around her neck, prancing around the parking lot and trying to provoke me. She refused to hand it over. So… I'm not gonna lie. I got upset and tried to remove it myself. Harper made a big scene. Started screaming and whatnot. The neighbor came outside and saw what was going on. Thought I was trying to choke Harper. So she called the police."

"Okay," Todd said, tapping his finger against the table. "That's uh…that's a lot. But let me ask you this. Why did Harper file the order of protection in the first place?"

"Because she'd found out about my affairs and got angry. So angry that she lied to the courts claiming that I'd been violent toward her. It was simply payback for my infidelity."

"My goodness…" Elle whispered, clasping her hands together.

Todd could tell by the look in her darting eyes that she was overwhelmed. Hell, he was, too. Keaton could be lying. But if so, he was damned good at it.

"What about the divorce settlement?" Todd asked. "Were you upset with the amount and fighting it in court?"

"I wasn't upset with the amount. I was concerned over what Harper planned to do with the money. I wanted her to invest it wisely, not blow it all trying to keep up with that women's group. I tried to work out some sort of monthly payment plan where she wouldn't receive the entire settlement at once. But Harper fought me on it, insisting she get it in one lump sum. That money would've been gone in less than a year."

"What about the scarf?" Elle asked. "Did you ever get it back?"

"I did. Eventually…"

Todd observed Keaton's demeanor once again. His posture was tall. Eye contact was direct. Nothing about him appeared deceptive.

"I'm glad we came here to meet with you," he said. "I had a completely different perspective on this situation before today. I think Elle and I both have a lot more clarity now."

"Good. I'm happy to hear that. Thank you for giving me the opportunity to tell my side of the story. Do you think anything I shared will help in your investigation?"

"Absolutely," Elle replied. "You've just confirmed that Todd and I are on the right path."

"The path to take down The Precious Jewels, I hope," Keaton said, slamming his hand down onto the table.

A worker came over and tapped him on the shoulder.

"We need you over by the main water fountain, boss. We're getting a slow trickle rather than a full flow."

Keaton grunted loudly. "Ugh. Sounds like a leak in the seal or the suction lines. I'll be over in a minute."

Todd stood and extended his hand. "We'll let you get back to work."

"Deputy Jacobson, Elle, thanks again. I look forward to reading all about how you two disbanded The Precious Jewels and threw the crooked members behind bars."

Todd smiled slyly while removing his hard hat. "Have a good afternoon."

He and Elle headed back to the car.

"Welp, that was pretty damn eye-opening," she said.

"It most certainly was. Now it's time to go even harder. Catch this killer before someone else loses their life."

Chapter Twenty-One

Elle sat at her parents' kitchen table, scrolling through the Cuban Cigar Specialty website. Last time she was at Todd's house, she'd noticed that his Spanish cedar humidor was practically empty. So she'd decided to surprise him with a box of Romeo y Julieta Wide Churchills for Christmas.

"You're buying Todd a *Christmas* gift?" Rachel had asked when Elle went to her for cigar recommendations.

"Yes. Why? What's the big deal?"

"What's the *big deal*? When was the last time you bought a Christmas gift for a man you weren't in love with?"

The question was valid. Elle had never bought a present for a man who wasn't her relative or significant other.

"Girl, please," was the only response she could come up with.

Elle wasn't ready to verbalize her feelings for Todd just yet. Plus she needed to remain focused on Taylor's investigation, not on making a love connection.

Just as she added the cigars to her cart, Elle's cell phone rang. She didn't recognize the number.

Oh no...

She reached for the phone, her hand jittery with apprehension.

"Hello?"

She winced at the quiver in her voice.

"Hello, Elle?"

"Yes?"

"This is Keaton. Keaton Mitchell."

"Ah," Elle sighed and slumped into the back of her chair. "Keaton, hey. What's going on?"

"I'm sorry to bother you. I tried phoning Todd but the call went straight to voice mail."

"He's down at the station in an all-day training session. Is there something I can help you with?"

"I hope so. I was going through some of Harper's things to donate to the Salvation Army, and I found a file that contained an interesting letter."

Elle stood up and walked over to the window. "What type of letter?"

"It was from her attorney. Apparently one of the women Harper had recruited into The Precious Jewels went to the IRS claiming that members were committing wire fraud and filing false tax returns."

"*Really.* So much for that sisterly bond."

"You should see all the emails, text messages and social media posts that the plaintiff turned over."

Elle put the call on speaker and began composing a text to Todd.

"Harper was in the process of cutting a deal with the feds. In exchange for providing information on Sloane Whitlock and Linda Basco, she would avoid jail time."

The phone almost fell from Elle's hands. "In the process, meaning she never cut the deal?"

"No. She didn't. She died the day before the meeting with the federal agent was scheduled to take place."

A cold chill swept over Elle. She tried to take a deep breath. But shock had blocked her airways.

"Can you send me a copy of that letter and the accompanying correspondence?" she asked. "I want to include it in the report that Todd and I are presenting to Sheriff Glover."

"Of course. Text me your email address. I'll get everything over to you ASAP."

The phone buzzed. Todd was calling on the other line.

"Keaton, I need to go. I'll keep an eye out for that information."

She swapped calls.

"Todd! Did you—"

"Yes. I just saw your text message. I had to excuse myself from the training session and I've only got a few minutes."

"Then I'll make this quick. We have got to take our case to Sheriff Glover. *Now.* Time is running out. If we don't see to it that The Precious Jewels are dismantled ASAP, they're going to end up killing each other until there's only one woman standing."

"I hear you, Elle. But we still don't have a smoking gun. I know I said I wanted to go to him sooner rather than later, but we have to have something nearly airtight when we do go. Glover won't listen otherwise. What direct evidence is there to argue our case? Clearly Sloane is using her high-power status to fly under law enforcement's radar. If Chloe is involved in this, she's taking advantage of that as well. I suggest we stay the course and keep our investigation going until we've got solid proof of guilt."

The chill Elle had been feeling transformed into heated frustration. "You know what? Maybe I need to wear a wire and set Sloane up so that she thinks I'm preparing to rat her out to the feds. Then when she comes after me, you can catch her in the act and arrest her."

"Hold on, hold on. The feds might be on this case right now if Harper was about to sit down with an agent," he said.

"If that were true, don't you think we would have picked up on it by now? If the feds are involved, they're moving at a snail's pace. C'mon, I can do this."

Todd sighed audibly. "You'll do it anyway, won't you?" he asked. "No matter what I say."

She smiled. "Yes."

"All right. Desperate times call for desperate measures…"

"Deputy Jacobson!" someone called out. "We need you back in here."

"Listen," Todd said, "I've gotta return to my session. Why don't you start brainstorming some ideas? I'll do the same. We'll reconvene tonight."

ELLE SLID A piece of salmon sashimi around on her plate. She and Todd were sitting in a far corner inside The Freshwater Grill. Todd was friends with the owner, so he'd allowed the pair to dine in a closed-off section of the restaurant for privacy.

"Here's what I'm thinking," Elle said. "I'll tell Sloane that I need to have a private, in-person conversation with her. When we meet up, I'll explain that a federal agent reached out to me asking if I'm a member of The Precious Jewels, what do I know about the group, etcetera etcetera. If Sloane asks, I'll use the same agent's name that was working with Harper—"

"But you won't mention knowing anything about the Harper situation, right?"

"Of course not. I won't make any mention of Harper at all."

"Good. And you'll wear a wire when you meet with Sloane?"

"Yes, I'll wear the wire, and we'll record the conversation. I can use the information that Harper gave her attorney and make it seem as if I received it from the federal agent. That should get her to talking."

Todd refilled their cups of sake. "And when she asks whether or not you're going to meet with the agent?"

"I'll tell her that I am. I'll share the date and time, too."

"Then that, my friend, will set the trap."

Elle raised her drink in the air. "It certainly will. Because on that day, Sloane will come after me, you'll go after her, and she will finally be arrested."

"Cheers to that," he said flatly.

They clinked their cups together and sipped their rice wine.

"You don't sound enthused," she said to him.

"I don't like using you as bait. It could be dangerous."

She smiled at his concern. "I'll be careful. And you'll be watching. And listening."

"I wish there was a better way."

"It's all we've got right now."

"And you'll do it even without my involvement," he said, as if the matter was settled.

"Let me ask you this," Elle said as she poured soy sauce over her dragon roll. "Where does Bryce stand in our investigation at this point? I mean, we're so focused on Sloane and The Precious Jewels. Is he still in this?"

"Absolutely. The Precious Jewels are just at the top of the suspects list. For the time being, let's focus on them, primarily Sloane. When she goes down, Chloe will automatically follow suit, and so will everyone else involved."

"The domino effect."

"Exactly."

Todd reached across the table and dabbed his napkin against the corner of Elle's mouth.

"Wasabi sauce," he said.

"Oh…" Her cheeks burned under his piercing gaze. "Thanks."

"I think we've had enough talk about the investigation for one night," Todd said. "Why don't we switch gears? Lighten up the mood a bit?"

"I'd like that. Because we have been talking about this case incessantly."

"That we have." Todd ran his fingertip along the rim of his cup. "So, have you heard from your ex?"

Elle almost choked on her sashimi. "Wait, is that what you call lightening the mood?"

He chuckled. "I guess not. I…uh… I was just curious. That's all."

"Well, to answer your question, no. I have not heard from my ex. As a matter of fact, a mutual friend told me he's already seeing someone else."

"Was that upsetting to hear?"

"Not really. It was just further proof that we didn't belong together. He never even tried to fight for our relationship. He just nonchalantly agreed when I suggested we part ways."

"Had he fought to keep you, would you have stayed?"

"No. Because I know there's better waiting out here for me."

"I couldn't agree more. And it just might be closer than you think."

Todd's cell phone buzzed. He and Elle held their gaze for several moments before he checked the text.

"Deputy Cross and some of the other deputies are heading over to Bradford High's football game. They're playing their biggest rival tonight."

"Duncan Tech?"

"Yep. You wanna go after we're done with dinner?"

Elle didn't immediately respond.

"I hear the marching band is gonna be playing Christmas carols during halftime," Todd continued. "Not to mention we could both use a break from all this investigative work."

"That's true. I haven't done anything just for fun since I've been back in Bradford."

"And Taylor would *not* be pleased with that. So, what do you say? Let's take a night off and go enjoy ourselves. Stuff our faces with churros and cheap chocolate candy bars like we used to do back in the day."

"You know what?" she said. "Yes. Let's go."

Chapter Twenty-Two

Elle pulled in front of Sloane's house. Checked the rearview mirror. Watched as Todd rounded the corner and pulled over at the end of the block.

Her cell phone rang. It was him.

"Hey," she said as he flashed his headlights. "I see you back there."

"Good. I'll be here the whole time. How are you feeling?"

"Nervous, but ready," Elle said, adjusting the collar on her suede lilac blazer.

Nervous was an understatement. Her heart thumped so forcefully that it practically rattled her silver chain necklace.

Nevertheless, it was showtime.

Time to face Sloane, one-on-one…

"Do you have the recording device secured inside your jacket?" Todd asked.

"I do," she said, patting her pocket. The slender recorder, which was two inches long and wide, was tucked deep inside. "I just get so anxious thinking Sloane might see it, or it might fall out, and she'll realize what I'm really up to."

"She won't. Just be cool, don't fidget with your blazer, and stick to the script. You'll be fine."

"Thanks for the encouragement." Elle glanced at the clock. It was five minutes to seven. "I'd better go on in. I don't wanna be late."

"Good luck. Like I said, I'll be right here when you come out."

Elle double-checked to make sure that the device was turned on, then stepped out of the car.

Just as she slammed the door shut, Chloe came bouncing out of Sloane's house.

What are you doing here?

Elle hadn't wanted anyone to know that she was meeting with Sloane privately. The Precious Jewels were messy, and they loved to gossip. Especially Chloe.

The less they knew, the better.

"Elle?" Chloe said. "Is that you?"

"Yes, it is me. Hi."

Chloe came sashaying toward her, looking like the quintessential sorority member in her pale pink petticoat-style dress and string of pearls. "Hey, girl, hey! What are you doing here?"

"I…um—I just need to talk to Sloane about…about tips on how to recruit new members."

"*What?* You should've just come to me! I'm like, the *queen* of recruitment. Plus, I'm your mentor. You're gonna have Sloane thinking I'm not fulfilling my leadership duties!"

Elle waved her off. "Please. I'm sure she won't think that. I hadn't seen you at the last couple of events, so I figured you were busy and didn't have the time."

"Listen, I'm never too busy to coach my mentees. I've been traveling a lot, but I will always make time for you. We can email, text, chat over video conference. Whatever you want."

"Thank you. I'll remember that next time."

Chloe glanced up at Sloane's front door. "I actually stopped by to check on our fearless leader after hearing about that epic meltdown she had at the last meeting. I wish I had been here. I feel like I could've done something to stop it."

"It was pretty bad. So bad that I don't think anyone could've stopped it. Linda certainly tried."

"Yeah, well, Linda's not me. She's weak." Chloe moved in closer. "Just between us, I'm hoping to knock her out of that number two spot. *Soon.* I've got a plan, too."

Elle's ears perked up. "You do?"

"I do. And I ran it by Sloane tonight. She liked it. I'll share the deets with you if you promise not to say anything."

"Of course I won't. It'll stay between us."

"Awesome. So, I asked Sloane if she'd like to co-host a tea party with me this weekend, which would be sponsored by The Precious Jewels. We'd invite a select group of prominent women from Bradford and a few surrounding counties. Nothing too fancy. Just something casual at Sloane's place. It'll be a push to recruit new members, and of course bring in more money."

"That sounds like a great idea, Chloe. I'm sure it'll help to lift Sloane's spirits, too."

Chloe bounced up and down on her high heels. "That is exactly what I was thinking! Of course we'll charge an entry fee, which is only fair considering how amazing it will be to have all these VIPs in one room together. Can you imagine all the networking opportunities? And the added bonus is Sloane and I are gonna make a huge profit off this."

"Oh, so…you and Sloane are going to split the proceeds among yourselves?"

Chloe's head bobbed from side to side. "I mean, we'll probably donate a small portion of it to charity. Which of course we'd write off on our taxes. Speaking of taxes, that's the beauty of being a Precious Jewel. I haven't had to report any of the money I've made to the IRS. So I'm just out here making a killing!"

Elle's eyes squinted as she watched Chloe readjust her rhinestone Chanel broach. "Wait, isn't that illegal?"

Chloe's lips curled into a knowing smirk. "I don't know. Is it?"

Sloane's porch light came on. Elle looked up the driveway. Ivory Chantilly lace curtains parted as she appeared in the window.

Elle pulled her cell out of her purse and checked the time. It was ten minutes after seven.

"Anyway," Chloe continued, "I just figured Sloane could use a boost since some of our fellow Jewels are questioning her involvement in those deaths. What better way to do that than to generate some cash—"

"Elle!" Sloane yelled from her veranda. "You're late! What are you doing out there?"

"Sorry! I'll be up in a sec."

Chloe grabbed Elle's shoulders and gave an air kiss on each cheek. "You'd better go. Be on the lookout for Sloane's tea party invitation. She's going to email it out tonight. It'll contain all the deets on the event. Be sure not to share it with anyone!"

"I won't. Thanks!"

When Elle reached the front door, she was greeted with an angry glare.

"The one thing you will not do," Sloane snarled, "is disrespect my time. My calendar is jam-packed, Elle. Yet I was gracious enough to clear a spot for you at the last minute. And what do you do? You insult me by—"

"Sloane, please," Elle interrupted. "I am so sorry. I was actually here on time. But I ran into Chloe on the way in, and we started chatting about all of the exciting things that are going on with The Precious Jewels. Time just got away from me. Again, my apologies."

Sloane stepped to the side and held out her hand. Elle entered the foyer reluctantly, feeling the angry heat coming off Sloane as she walked past her.

Elle was surprised to see her dressed in yet another velour leisure suit, this one a pale shade of yellow. From the looks of her loose ponytail and bare face, Sloane was still in meltdown mode.

"Excuse is the tool of the incompetent," Sloane said while leading them into the great room.

What in the hell is this woman talking about?

"A monument of nothingness," she continued. "And those that use it are not wise. Have you heard that quote, Elle?"

"No. I have not."

"Words to live by, spoken by Pastor Paul Adefarasin. Keep them in mind *the next time you run late for a meeting with me then make excuses for it.* Now, have a seat and tell me what's so urgent that you *insisted on coming here* on such short notice."

The glare in Sloane's steely eyes made Elle want to get up and leave. Her dark aura was chilling. Elle felt as though she was looking into the face of a killer.

Time to take you down...

Elle cleared her throat. "I wanted to let you know that I received a call from a federal agent."

Sloane's scowl fell into an open-mouthed gape.

"Wh-what did he want?" she asked, her overly plumped bottom lip quivering. "What did he say?"

Elle felt her body relax. She crossed her legs, unable to resist finding pleasure in Sloane's fear.

"*She*. The agent is a woman."

"Okay. What did *she* want?"

"To know whether or not I'm a member of The Precious Jewels."

Sloane slapped her hands against her thighs. "*And?* What did you tell her?"

"I told her that I am."

"*Dammit*, Elle!"

Sloane jumped up and began walking in circles, her UGG slippers sliding across the white glass mosaic tiles.

"What else did she ask?"

"Um...let me think," Elle stalled. She bounced her knees rapidly, feigning nervousness. "She asked whether or not I was required to pay an initiation fee in order to join."

"What'd you say?"

"That I was."

"Ahh!" Sloane spun around and fell against the quartz fireplace mantel. "You are killing me, Elle! Are you that daft? Why the hell would you tell her that?"

"Because it's the truth! And I—I was nervous. Plus they're the *feds*, Sloane. They already know the answers to their questions before they even ask them."

Sloane dropped her head and turned her back to

Elle. "First Harper and now you," she muttered under her breath.

"Wait, what did you just say?" Elle asked, hoping that her recorder had picked up the comment.

"I said, first Harper, and now you!" Sloane pivoted and rushed toward Elle, her wide eyes darting with fury.

Elle recoiled, gripping the arm of the couch.

"You'd better not speak another word about The Precious Jewels," Sloane spewed. "To anyone!"

"So…so what am I supposed to tell this agent when I meet with her?"

A guttural howl pierced Elle's ears. She thought it'd come from one of Sloane's dogs. But it had come from her.

"*Meet* with her? You actually agreed to meet with the feds, Elle? To discuss *my* organization?"

"Yes, of course! What was I supposed to do? Tell them no?"

"When is the meeting?"

"Next week. Monday. At nine a.m. to be exact."

Sloane grabbed Elle's arm and yanked her off the couch.

"Ouch!" Elle shrieked, stunned by the petite woman's strength.

"Get out," Sloane insisted as she dragged Elle toward the door. "Get the hell out of my house! Expect a call from my attorney first thing in the morning. And if you speak one word about The Precious Jewels to a single soul, I swear I will sue you for slander and take everything you own. Not that it appears to be much."

Sloane threw open the door, then leaned in so closely that Elle could smell the whiskey on her breath. "I do not go down without a fight. And I never fought a battle I didn't win."

"Wh-what do you mean by that?"

"Take it however you want. Now get out!"

Sloane pushed Elle onto the veranda and slammed the door.

Elle just stood there, breathing heavily, struggling to regain her composure. And then, she broke into a fit of elated laughter.

"I just got everything I need, and then some."

She hurried down the driveway and stared down the street in search of Todd's car. It wasn't there.

That's strange...

Elle pulled out her cell phone to dial his number. When she unlocked the screen, a text message from him appeared.

Hey, there was a robbery over at Ingram's Grab N Go. Deputy Cross asked me to meet him there and check out the scene. I should be back at Sloane's before your meeting ends. So hang tight. I'll be back soon.

"Yeah, not gonna happen," Elle muttered to herself as she responded to the message.

Things at Sloane's didn't go as planned. Long story short, she kicked me out. I'll just head back to my parents' house. Meet me there when you're done. I'll tell you all about it then.

Elle sent the message and hopped inside her car.

She started the engine and slowly pulled away from the curb. A pair of headlights flashed behind her. She called Todd to see if it was him. The call went straight to voice mail.

Elle drove to the corner and stopped. A twinge of queasiness pierced her stomach.

Something didn't feel right.

She glanced in the rearview mirror. Darkness blanketed the street. The car's headlights had been turned off.

The tension in Elle's joints slackened.

Stop allowing your imagination to get the best of you. You're fine. No one is following you...

She turned down Austin Lane and sped through a yellow light. Glanced in the side-view mirror. The road was empty.

"See? You're good."

Elle switched on the satellite radio and turned to the twenty-four-hour Christmas jazz station. Duke Ellington's rendition of "Jingle Bells" piped through the speakers. She bobbed her head to the beat of his lively remake while heading into downtown.

A traffic controller resembling a slightly taller Danny DeVito stopped her as she approached Livingston Avenue. She rolled down the window.

"What's going on?"

"Happy holidays, ma'am. We closed off the street for the Taste of Christmas Carnival."

"The *what*?"

"The Taste of Christmas Carnival. It's something new that the restaurant owners are doing this year. Everybody's cooking up their most popular holiday dishes and serving them at individual booths all along Livingston Ave. You should do yourself a favor and check it out, especially Patty's merry mac and cheese—"

"I'm sorry," Elle interrupted, "but I'm gonna have to miss out this year. I really need to get home. Is there a detour I can take?"

"Where are you headed?"

"Kenwood Street."

"Oh, that's easy. Just head over to Oak Lane and cut through Everest Forest Preserve. That'll get you to Kenwood in no time."

Elle's jaws clenched. She thought back on the moment that black pickup truck rammed into her car at the forest preserve.

Just pull over. Wait for Todd to finish up at Ingram's...

A horn blew behind her.

"Give me a minute, will you?" Elle yelled out the window.

The traffic controller tapped her door frame. "I'm sorry, ma'am. But I'm gonna have to ask you to either pull into the parking lot or take the detour. You're holding up traffic."

Stop being paranoid. Just take the detour and get home. You'll be fine.

Elle made a U-turn and headed toward Oak Lane. She stopped at a red light and tried calling Todd again. It went straight to voice mail again.

"Hey, it's Elle," her voice quaked.

Shake it off...

"Wanted to let you know that Livingston Avenue is closed off for an event. I'm being rerouted through the Everest Forest Preserve. So...um...yeah. Just thought I should share that. Hope everything's okay at Ingram's and no one got hurt. I can't wait to tell you about the craziness that happened at Sloane's. Call me back. Or, if you can't, I'll see you at my parents' house or whatever."

You're rambling. Hang up the phone.

The light turned green. Elle disconnected the call and glanced in the rearview mirror. No one was behind her.

She hit the accelerator and made a right turn into the forest preserve.

"Come on, Todd. Call me back."

Hearing his voice would help calm her nerves. Convince her that she was overreacting.

Elle turned down the radio as if that would help, then switched on her bright lights. She checked the side-view mirror. No one was there.

"See? You just being—"

She paused when a car appeared behind her.

Relax. It's a public thoroughfare. Other people are allowed to drive on it.

The vehicle remained at a safe distance.

Elle focused on the road ahead. Safe distance or not, she was desperate to get to the other side.

The lampposts that were sporadically placed along the street appeared to be out. The forest preserve felt more like an abysmal black tunnel than a roadway. There didn't appear to be an end in sight.

But you know that there is. Just get to the other side.

Elle was hit with an eerie sense of vulnerability. The massive evergreen trees looming overhead took her breath away. They felt monstrous. As if they were closing in on her.

The car behind her had the same effect as it got closer. And closer.

Not again. No. Not again!

She slammed down on the accelerator until it hit the floorboard. Her car jolted forward, flying through the darkness.

Elle could barely see what was up ahead. She didn't care. She was determined to escape her attacker this time.

Headlights flashed in her rearview mirror. The car tailing her sped up. Its engine roared loudly as the horn blew erratically.

"What in the hell are you doing?" Elle screamed. "Leave me alone!"

Elle drove faster. The vehicle behind her followed suit.

Fears of a deer or fallen tree in the road crossed her mind. Elle pushed out the thoughts.

Just focus on the other side. Focus on the other side.

Her cell phone rang. It was Todd.

She pounded the Bluetooth button.

"Todd! I'm being chased through the forest preserve again!"

"Stay calm, Elle. I got your voice mail and I'm heading that way now. Are you still on Oak Lane?"

"Yes! Please hurry. Somebody is trying to run me off the road!"

The headlights shone so brightly behind her that Elle could barely see up ahead.

"Hang on. I'm almost there. Can you tell what type of vehicle it is?"

"No," she whimpered. "It's too dark. All I can see is lights."

"Okay. Stay on the line. I'm turning down Oak Lane now. You're heading north toward your parents' house, right?"

"Yes," she breathed, her eyes darting back and forth between the rearview mirror and the road.

The car wasn't letting up. The faster she drove, the closer it got.

"I see lights up ahead," Todd said. "I'm coming up the rear."

"Please hurry!"

"I'm catching up. Listen, I want to pin this car in between us. So, start slowing down."

Elle sat up in her seat, craning her neck in search of him. "Are you sure?"

"I'm positive. I can see your car. Just trust me. Start letting up on the accelerator."

Please let this work…

She said a quick prayer, then gradually lifted her foot off the pedal. The car chasing her slowed down.

"You see that side road up ahead?" Todd asked.

"I do."

"Make a quick right. It's a one way. We'll jam this maniac in between our cars."

"Okay."

Elle quickly steered her car down the road. Sure enough, the vehicle followed.

"I'm right behind you two," Todd said. "Keep going about a hundred more feet, then stop."

"I am so nervous," she said, her stomach churning uncontrollably.

"Just stay calm. You got this. Okay, now…stop!"

Elle slammed down on the brakes. The car behind her came to an abrupt halt, inches away from her bumper.

Todd jumped out of his vehicle and approached the attacker's door.

"Get out of the car with your hands up!" he yelled with his gun and flashlight drawn.

Elle spun around in her seat, anxious to see who would step out of the unfamiliar burgundy sedan.

The door slowly opened. A bare leg swung out. A nude Mary Jane pump hit the dirt.

Who the…

Elle's hand trembled as she pulled the door handle. She stepped outside, watching Todd move toward the suspect.

The woman climbed out of the car. Todd flashed the light in her face.

It was Chloe.

"Elle!" she squealed. "I hope I didn't scare you."

Elle marched toward her, stunned.

"What the hell do you mean, *you hope you didn't scare me*? Of course you did! Why are you chasing me through the forest preserve?"

Chloe turned to Todd. "Um, excuse me. But could you please put that gun away and stop shining that light in my face?"

"Not until you tell us what you're doing."

She reached inside of her car.

"Keep your hands where I can see them, Chloe!" Todd warned.

She stood back up and handed him something.

"What is that?" Elle asked, taking a step toward her.

"Your debit card. You dropped it while we were standing outside of Sloane's house."

Elle almost fell to her knees. *"Chloe,"* she snapped, snatching the card. "You went through all of that just to return this?"

"Of course! I didn't want you looking for it, then

panicking when you couldn't find it. I waited outside of Sloane's house for you instead of knocking since she was so angry that you were late. Then you left so soon after you got there that I wasn't able to catch you."

"Yeah, that's because she kicked me out."

"She did? Why?"

Elle paused. She glanced over at Todd, who discreetly shook his head.

"Long story," Elle told her. "Anyway, now that I've recovered from the massive heart attack you just induced, I need to get out of here. Thank you for returning my card."

"You're welcome. Sorry for the scare."

Todd wrapped his arm around Elle. "Are you okay?"

She inhaled sharply, leaning into his chest. "I will be. I just wanna go home and relax. Shake this whole experience off."

"Understood. I'll follow you and make sure you get there safely."

"Would you mind staying with me for a while?"

"Of course not. I'll stay with you for as long as you want."

The intensity in his lively eyes told Elle that he wasn't just referring to that night.

"Aww, look at the two *lovebirds*," Chloe sang. "How cute."

Todd threw her a look. "Be safe getting home, Chloe."

"Oh, wait, no police escort for me, too?"

"I'll make sure you get back out onto the main road safely," he replied through tight lips before turning back to Elle. "Hey, I'm so sorry I missed your calls earlier. I couldn't get any reception inside of Ingram's. This should have never—"

"You do not owe me an apology, Todd. This was my fault. I should've just waited for you. But you got here right on time."

"Thank God it was a false alarm. Now let's get out of here."

Chapter Twenty-Three

Elle handed Todd a mug of hot chocolate topped with whipped cream and cinnamon.

"Ooh, that looks so fancy. Thank you."

"Hold on. I'm not done yet."

She grabbed two candy canes from her mother's crystal snowflake-shaped bowl and slid them inside their mugs. "Now it's really fancy."

The pair were back at Elle's parents' place, relaxing on the tan leather couch inside the family room.

She'd lit the brick fireplace as soon as they had arrived, to take the chill out of the air. Its flames crackled softly in the background. A large evergreen wreath hung over the mantel, the scent of its pine cones wafting through the air.

Being back at the Scotts' house felt warm and tranquil, now that the broken furniture had been removed and replaced, and the home cleaned from top to bottom, insurance covering it all. Elle had just moved back in, he knew, while her parents stayed with friends for a while.

Being in Elle's presence felt like home.

Todd was glad to see that she had finally calmed down after the evening's fiasco.

"Mmm," he said after taking a sip of hot chocolate. "It tastes as good as it looks."

"Thank you. Have you forgotten that Taylor and I mastered the art of crafting hot chocolate during our junior year of high school? That's when we started selling it out of my parents' garage."

"Really? No, I don't remember that. I must've been on one of my massive workout-slash-healthy-eating binges that year. Otherwise I would've guzzled your entire supply before anyone could buy a cup."

Elle threw her head back and laughed. Todd gazed at her. She still appeared radiant, despite her traumatic night.

Loose curls framed her smiling face. A faint trace of pink gloss covered her supple lips.

Todd felt the urge to lean in and kiss them. But he resisted. The romantic gesture didn't seem fitting in the moment.

"So Sloane put you out of her house, huh?" Todd asked.

"Like Martin did Pam on almost every episode of his sitcom."

"Ha! I'm glad you're able to joke about it."

"Sometimes you just gotta laugh to keep from crying, right?"

Todd gave her arm an affectionate nudge. "Ah, come on. There's no crying in criminal justice. We are so close to solving this case, Elle. You were great tonight. You did what you set out to do. Planted the seed in Sloane's mind that you're meeting with a federal agent."

"Yeah, but I'm not gonna lie. That run-in with Chloe at the forest preserve has me shaken up. I know it was a false alarm and all, but it gave me a taste of what may happen if Sloane comes after me. That was scary."

"I know it was. But the difference is I won't leave your side next time. Getting called to Ingram's was an unexpected fluke. No matter what comes my way the day of your fake meeting with the feds, I'll be there. Period. Got it?"

"Got it." Elle stared down at her cup, poking at the whipped cream with her candy cane. "You know, it just dawned on me that Chloe wasn't driving her Range Rover tonight. I've never seen that car she was in before. I wonder who it belongs to. And where's her truck?"

"Good question. I was so discombobulated by all the chaos that I didn't think to ask. Maybe you can find out when you see her at that Precious Jewels tea party this weekend."

"I will. That should be an interesting event. We'll see if Sloane can get back to her normal, glamorous self. Maybe she'll show up in something besides a tracksuit and avoid having another meltdown."

"I would hope so since it sounds like she's inviting the who's who among all of North Carolina."

Elle dug inside of her pocket and pulled out the recording device.

"Damn," Todd said. "In the midst of all the madness, I forgot that you recorded your conversation with Sloane. Did you get any useful information?"

"Nothing that could land her in jail. She did mention Harper being contacted by the feds. And said something about not going down without a fight. The juiciest bites were of her freaking out over my meeting with the federal agent."

"I guess you got kicked out before you could really dig for some dirt."

"Exactly."

Todd gently swiped a lock of hair away from Elle's eye. "Is it okay if I shift gears for a minute? Talk about something outside of the case?"

Elle turned, her lips brushing slightly against the palm of his hand. "Of course."

He took a long sip of his hot chocolate. "How do you feel being back in Bradford? I mean, aside from working Taylor's case. Are you enjoying spending time in your hometown?"

Elle sat back, her head tilting to the side.

"You know, I am. I live a fast-paced life in New York City. Being back here has reminded me that there's an easier pace. One that may be better suited for me now that I'm getting older and tired of that jet-setting lifestyle."

"Hmm, interesting. I'm sure it helps that you've returned during the holidays. I don't know about you, but as far as I'm concerned, there's no place in the world that does Christmas quite like Bradford."

"Oh, I totally agree. There's something about this town during the season that can't be replicated. The warm sense of community coming together to curate all these amazing events. The unique, handcrafted decorations and elaborate lights festivals. And don't even get me started on the delicious food. It literally feels like the most wonderful time of the year around here."

Todd slid closer toward her. "It does. Especially this year, having you home. This has been nice. Really nice. The time we've spent together has been primarily about Taylor, but being around you just feels…*good*."

"Thank you, Todd. I feel the same way about you. But…there's something that I have to ask."

"Ask away."

Elle pulled at a string hanging from the couch cushion. "What about your ex? Is there a chance that you two might get back together?"

Todd shook his head adamantly. "No. Absolutely not. That relationship had run its course. I've been looking forward to the next chapter in my life ever since."

"Have you been dating since the breakup?"

He set his hot chocolate down and tugged at his sweater sleeve, avoiding eye contact.

"Wait, what are you doing?" Elle asked. Her shrill tone was filled with amusement. "Did I hit a nerve asking that question?"

Todd smiled sheepishly. "Maybe…"

"Okay. Spill it. What type of dating disasters have you gotten yourself into? At least give me one good story."

Todd fell against the back of the couch and covered his face. "Man, I do have some stories to tell. But the wildest one has got to be the time I connected with a woman who lives in Florida through a dating app."

"Wait, you've tried online dating?"

"I have. And it was a nightmare. But let's not dwell on that. I'll just hurry up and share this *one* story so that we can hurry up and change the subject."

"Okay, fine. Let's hear it."

"So I met this woman who lived in Tampa. We clicked immediately. We'd text, talk on the phone and video-chat whenever we could. After about a month of that, I decided to fly to Tampa and meet her in person."

Elle snickered into her hand. "Oh no. Please don't tell me you went all the way to Florida and got catfished."

"No, no. I didn't. When I met her in person, she looked exactly like her photos."

"So, what went wrong?"

"Well, after an amazing seafood dinner at Ocean Prime, then a wine tasting on the Tampa Riverwalk, I was ready to call it a night. But my date had other plans. She insisted that we stop by one last spot before I went back to my hotel…"

Todd's voice trailed off. He stared up at the ceiling, clenching his teeth together.

"Hey, you can't just leave me hanging like that!" Elle insisted. "Come on. Finish the story."

"Ugh," Todd groaned. "The memory of it all just turns my stomach." He sat back up. "So anyway, after this woman begged and pleaded, I agreed to go to this one last spot. I pull up to the address and see that it's a private residence. We go around to the back of the house, enter through a sliding glass door, and are led to the basement by a woman dressed in all black leather from head to toe. Oh, and she was wearing a cape, too."

"A *cape*?"

"Yes. A cape."

"What was this, some type of costume party?"

"Not quite. When we got down to the basement, I realized that it was a swinger party."

"Excuse me," Elle said, turning her ear toward Todd. "It was a what?"

"A *swinger party*."

"Oh my word. I have heard it all. What happened next?"

"I got the hell outta there, that's what happened next. My date insisted on staying, so I left her there. Flew back home the next day and never spoke to her again."

"*Wow.* If this were a dating disaster competition, you'd win first place. Hands down."

"Thanks. I think…" he said before finishing off his hot chocolate. "Lucky for me, the days of random dating are behind me now. I've taken myself off the market."

"Really? Why?"

"Because I'm done wasting my time. Until the real thing comes along, I'm cool just being single."

"That's understandable. I feel the same way."

Elle yawned, stretching her arms high in the air.

"Looks like somebody is getting sleepy," Todd said.

"I am. But I'm also really enjoying your company."

"Same here. But it's getting late. And we've had a long, challenging day. We should probably get some rest."

"We should." Elle stood and held out her hand. "I'll walk you to the door."

Todd took her hand in his and followed her to the living room.

Her tender touch was soothing. It made him think twice about going home and sleeping alone.

"I'll call you tomorrow," she said.

"Please do."

Todd leaned down and kissed her gently on the forehead. She gazed up at him, then pressed her mouth against his. He closed his eyes, relishing the feel of her soft lips.

Todd felt his jeans tighten near the zipper. He quickly pulled away and opened the door.

"Talk to you tomorrow," he said, rushing out the door.

Chapter Twenty-Four

Elle looked around Sloane's great room. It was packed with some of the wealthiest and most uppity women she had ever seen.

The Precious Jewels tea party was in full swing. Despite the last-minute email invitation that Sloane sent out, she'd gotten a huge turnout.

The room was filled with a sea of perfectly coiffed bouffant hairstyles, designer duds, pricey handbags and surgically enhanced faces. Conversations ranged from summer home purchases to husbands' affairs, booming businesses to gossip on who'd filed for bankruptcy.

Elle could not have felt more out of place. Her feet were beginning to ache inside her spiked-heel ankle boots, which she shouldn't have worn considering they hadn't been broken in yet.

She let out a deep breath just as Rachel walked back over and handed her a porcelain teacup.

"One pumpkin spice tea with a dash of raw sugar for you, and one peppermint tea with two packets of stevia for me."

"Thank you, ma'am."

"So why are you standing over here looking so disgusted?" Rachel asked.

"You know, I'm getting tired of being around all these superficial, overbearing women. And I don't feel comfortable being back inside this house after Sloane kicked me out the other day. I know that none of this is real, and I'm working undercover to solve Taylor's murder. But this entire situation is getting to me. I'm ready for it to be over."

"Well, from what I can tell, you and Todd are almost there. So keep going, sis. You got this."

"I hope so." Elle tugged at the collar of her plain black A-line dress. "I feel so underdressed next to all these other women. Chloe said this party would be casual."

Rachel stepped back and pointed at her denim jumpsuit. "Yeah, tell me about. And look at Sloane. Is she about to serve as somebody's bride in that gold silk mermaid dress?"

Elle snickered. "Looks like it. She's doing way too much. I guess she finally snapped out of that slump she'd been in. I was expecting to see her in yet another velour tracksuit."

"Same. And her little sidekick Chloe's been flitting around here like she's the belle of the ball."

"Yeah, she's making her bid to take over Linda's spot," Elle said before taking a sip of tea.

"Well, it appears to be working. Sloane and the rest of these women are eating up her little corny jokes and kiss-ass compliments."

"Speaking of the devil, here she comes…"

Chloe came strolling toward the women, her powder blue cocktail dress swaying from side to side.

"Hello, ladies," she purred. "I'm glad you two were

able to make it. I love that my mentees are showing so much enthusiasm."

"You know us," Rachel said. "We're all about female empowerment, which The Precious Jewels clearly embodies."

Elle almost snorted at her sarcasm.

"Good," Chloe gushed. "That means we must be doing something right."

The group fell silent. Elle racked her brain for something to say. But her mind was blocked. Being around Chloe was triggering an odd sense of discomfort.

Maybe you're still not over that incident at the forest preserve...

Chloe turned toward her.

"Sooo, how are your recruiting efforts coming along?"

"They're…uh…they're coming along great. As a matter of fact, Rachel and I met several women at Pilar Samuels's art opening that are interested in joining The Precious Jewels."

"Oh, really? That is awesome! Have you invited them to our upcoming social yet?"

"We were planning on sending out invitations this week," Rachel chimed in. "Elle and I are determined to work our way up to Diamond status and cash out on that treasure chest. Right, E?"

"Absolutely."

Chloe squealed and bounced on her tippy toes. "Ah, this is all music to my ears!" She twirled around and then took a bow. On the way back up, she turned her ankle. "Ouch!"

Elle grabbed her arm. "Are you okay?"

"I think so," she said, bending down and rubbing her shin. "But I'd better go and sit down for a minute.

Take the weight off. I'd hate to end up with a fractured fibula like our girl Taylor."

Elle almost dropped her drink. "You'd—you'd *what*?"

"Let's reconvene later, ladies. My ankle is on fire," Chloe said before hobbling toward the couch.

"Elle?" Rachel said. "Why do you look like you just saw a demon?"

"Because I think I just did."

"What are you talking about?"

Elle turned to Rachel, so rattled that her teeth were chattering. "No one knew about Taylor's fractured fibula except for law enforcement. That information was never revealed to the public."

Rachel's head dropped. "Excuse me?"

"The sheriff's department only revealed that Taylor suffered an accidental neck injury."

Elle pulled out her cell phone and began texting Todd. "That's it. I'm over this. Todd has got to speak with Sheriff Glover about Taylor's case. Between Chloe, Sloane and Bryce, one of them killed her. And they need to find out who."

"Hell, at this point, maybe all three of them were involved."

"I'm asking Todd if he can try and talk the sheriff into bringing them all in for questioning. I mean, seriously, how much more evidence do we need to show that they are viable suspects? Just pull out the lie detector test so we can get to the truth!"

"Amen, sister. But considering all the political crap that goes on in this town? Good luck with that—"

Rachel was interrupted by the sound of a finger tapping against a microphone.

"Testing, testing, one-two, testing, one-two."

They turned to the front of the room. Sloane was standing at the podium with Linda to her right and Chloe to her left.

"I guess Chloe wasn't too injured to run up to her fearless leader," Elle muttered.

"Hello, ladies," Sloane said. "Welcome to The Precious Jewels' first annual holiday tea party. I am aware that you all lead such big, busy lives, which is why I'm so grateful that you took the time to celebrate the season with us."

The group gave Sloane a polite round of applause.

"This event is such an extraordinary networking opportunity," Sloane continued. "I'm trusting that you've all had a chance to mingle, converse and exchange contact information. More importantly, I hope that each of you has spoken to the members of The Precious Jewels and gotten to know more about our illustrious organization."

As Sloane schmoozed the crowd, Chloe pulled out her cell phone and began typing away.

"I'm sorry," Rachel whispered, "but could Chloe be any ruder? She is literally texting someone during the middle of Sloane's speech!"

"Um, have you met Chloe? She doesn't care about anyone except herself. She's just glad to be standing up there next to her idol. Next she'll be trying to knock Sloane out of her spot and take over The Precious Jewels."

Sloane leaned into the mic and cleared her throat. "I would love to introduce to you my cochair of this event, Chloe Hale. But it looks like there's something more important going on with that cellular phone of hers!"

The partygoers burst out laughing.

"Oh, no, no!" Chloe insisted, dropping her phone down by her side. "My apologies, Sloane. Please, go ahead."

"Thank you. Ladies, Chloe is one of the most dynamic members of The Precious Jewels that you could ever meet. She is ambitious, caring, and most importantly, *loyal*. As we all know, that is a hard trait to come by these days."

Sloane shot Elle a look.

Elle stared back at her, crossing her arms defiantly.

"Showdown at the Whitlock estate," Rachel hissed, struggling to contain her laughter.

"From Chloe's community service efforts to her passion toward our sisterhood," Sloane continued, "this woman's dedication to our organization is unmatched. She has made quite an impact on the Bradford community, as well as a ton of money, thanks to The Precious Jewels!"

Everyone broke into laughter once again.

"Oh, come on, Sloane," Chloe said, embracing her tightly. "You're too much. You're simply *too much*!"

"Ugh, I think I'm about to barf," Rachel said.

"So," Sloane said, "without further ado, I present to you one of The Precious Jewels' brightest stars, and a woman I'm proud to call my sister, Miss Chloe Hale!"

Cheers and applause filled the room while Chloe stepped up to the podium.

Elle rolled her eyes. "Here we go. This woman has been waiting for this moment all her life."

"Thank you so much for that wonderful introduction, Sloane! My goodness. How could I ever top that?" She held her finger to her chin and stared up at the ceiling. "Oh! I know. By telling you who I really am.

My name isn't Chloe Hale. It's Kendra Duval. And I'm not a member of The Precious Jewels. I am a special agent with the Federal Bureau of Investigations. Sloane Whitlock, Linda Basco, you are both under arrest for defrauding the IRS."

Audible gasps swept through the crowd. Elle grabbed hold of Rachel as her knees gave way.

"Am I losing my mind," Elle shrieked, "or did Chloe just say she's with the FBI?"

"No, *Kendra* just said she's with the FBI."

Elle's breathing grew shallow. "This is too much. I think I'm about to pass out…"

"Don't you dare fall out on me and miss all this good action!"

Sloane whimpered as Kendra, formerly known as Chloe, spun her around and put her in handcuffs.

"You—you *traitor*!" Sloane screamed. "How could you betray me like this?"

Kendra ignored her, remaining stone-faced as she moved on to handcuffing Linda.

Sloane's housekeeper came rushing into the great room, followed by several FBI agents.

"Mrs. Whitlock!" she yelled. "I tried to stop them, but they just came bursting through the door like a herd of *animals*!"

"Agent Keller!" Kendra yelled across the room. "Can you please take over the arrests? I need to show the other agents where they can find Mrs. Whitlock's computer and files."

"Absolutely, Agent Duval."

Two of the other agents began directing guests out of the house.

"Okay, ladies, the party's over. We're gonna have to ask you to leave. Please do so as quickly as possible."

Elle and Rachel clung to each other as women rushed past them, their faces twisted in horror and their high heels screeching across the tile.

"Look at all these guilty women," Rachel said. "Charging out of here before they get arrested, too."

Elle held her hand to her spinning head. "This is unreal. I cannot believe that Chloe... I mean *Kendra* is a special agent!"

"Yep. She is. And it looks like she's heading our way."

Kendra walked over and extended her hand. "Ladies, please, let me formally introduce myself. As you just heard, I'm special agent Kendra Duval, and I've been investigating The Precious Jewels over the past year." She handed Elle a business card. "I get the impression that you're really here to find out what happened to Taylor. Am I correct?"

"Yes. You are."

"I thought so. I assigned to this case in order to investigate the organization's suspected tax and wire fraud activity. But that doesn't mean Sloane's crimes stop there." She looked over her shoulder at the retreating crowd of shocked women. "We did this publicly to send a message to the rest of the Jewels. We might shake some informers out of the group." Her eyes focused once again on Elle. "I do think that you and Deputy Jacobson are on to something."

"Wait, you know about that?"

"Of course I do. Let's stay in touch. I'll be reaching out to Sheriff Glover as well."

"*Good*. Maybe all this will convince him to reopen Taylor's case." Elle paused, tapping Kendra's card against her palm. "You know, for a minute there, I thought that you might be the killer."

"I know you did. That was intentional. If you thought I was a murderer, you'd never suspect me of being a special agent."

"Agent Duval?" someone called out. "We need you in the library."

"I'll be there in a second!" She turned to Elle and Rachel. "Ladies, take care."

Kendra walked away, her usual peppy gait transforming into a stern stride.

"Do you see this?" Rachel asked. "That woman just sauntered off like Keyser Söze in *The Usual Suspects*."

"I do. And just like that character in the movie, Kendra had me completely fooled."

Elle stepped back as Sloane and Linda were led outside, both blabbering about their innocence through mascara-soaked tears.

"And now," Elle continued, "I don't have to put myself at risk by faking that meeting with the feds on Monday—"

She was interrupted by her buzzing cell phone. It was a text message from Todd.

Hey, I think calling Sloane and Chloe down to the station for questioning is a great idea, followed by Bryce. I'll go run it by Sheriff Glover and let you know what he says. How are things going at the tea party?

"Oh no. I've gotta call Todd and update him on what just happened here!" Elle said before grabbing Rachel's arm and rushing out the door.

Chapter Twenty-Five

Elle stood along the edge of the River Birch Park hiking trail. She'd gone there on a whim, motivated by Todd's plan to interrogate Bryce down at the station that evening.

After Sloane's and Linda's arrests, Sheriff Glover had finally agreed to reopen Taylor's case. He wanted to take a look at all possible suspects, including Bryce.

Elle had forgotten how quickly the sun set on December days. Gone was the dusky lavender sky that was present during her ride to the park. It had been replaced by blankets of heavy, gray clouds.

The scattered lampposts that lined the trail had been turned off. The park district must've assumed that the town's holiday-obsessed community would rather go ice skating or Christmas shopping than take a jog along the chilly trail.

And they would be right...

The trail was empty. And now dark.

Elle pulled a flashlight from her green nylon backpack and turned it up to the brightest setting. She was beginning to second-guess her rash decision to go out there. But she couldn't quiet her urge to revisit Taylor's crime scene once again.

Elle was still determined to uncover some sort of direct evidence linked to Taylor's murder. And now that Sloane was behind bars, Chloe had come out as a special agent and Bryce was at the sheriff's office, she felt safe knowing all their suspects were accounted for.

Elle approached the tulip tree near where Taylor's body had been found. She shined the flashlight toward the base of its trunk, studying the deep grooves in the brown, furrowed bark and inhaling its sweet, musky scent.

Elle wondered what had gone through Taylor's mind as she was being attacked in that very spot.

Why didn't you leave us a clue, friend? A clump of hair. Smear of blood. Set of footprints...

A blast of chilly wind blew straight through Elle's pink yoga jacket. She bowed her head and pulled the zipper toward her chin. The gust blew a small pile of dried orange leaves away from the tree trunk. They landed near Elle's gray sneakers, then swirled through the air as if caught in a tornado.

The spot that the leaves evacuated was covered in a cluster of twigs. Elle focused her light on the shoots.

One of them caught her eye. She took a step closer. It appeared to be covered in droplets of deep burgundy stains.

It couldn't be... Could it?

Elle's entire body began to shake. She bent down, her breathing quickening at the thought of finally uncovering a piece of evidence.

Her cell phone rang. She jumped up, almost falling backward from the shrill buzz.

"Calm down, girl," she told herself, accepting the call without bothering to check the caller ID.

"Elle Scott speaking."

"Hey," Todd said. "Are you okay?"

"I'm more than okay. I'm ecstatic. I think I just found a piece of evidence out at River Birch Park."

"River Birch Park? Elle, it's practically pitch-black outside! What are you doing out there? *Alone* no less?"

She pulled a pair of gloves and a plastic baggie out of her backpack.

"I know, I know. It wasn't this dark when I came out here. I felt compelled to revisit the crime scene while you were interrogating Bryce. Something was urging me to take another look. And I'm glad I did. Because guess what I see?"

"What?"

"A stick that looks to be covered in blood."

"Wait, you found *what*?"

"A twig, speckled in blood!" she repeated while slipping her hands inside the gloves.

"Are you sure, Elle? We combed that entire area several times over and came up empty on every occasion."

"I'm telling you what I see. I'll collect it, and you can send it off to the forensics lab for testing. If the stick is in fact connected to Taylor's murder, then that means my instincts were right. I was called to come out here for a reason."

"We'll see…"

Elle could tell by the sound of his low tone that Todd wasn't pleased. But she didn't care. Her actions would be justified if the potential evidence helped solve their case.

Elle's fingers trembled as she picked up the twig and slowly placed it inside the baggie.

"Got it," she declared, securing it inside her backpack.

Elle paused.

"Hold on, Todd. Shouldn't you be questioning Bryce right now?"

"Yes, I should be. That's why I was calling. To tell you that he didn't show up."

"What?"

"Bryce never came to the station. I called, texted and emailed him. Even sent a squad car by his house to see if he was there. He wasn't."

"That is so weird. One thing about Bryce, he's always been dependable. I wonder why he—"

She stopped midsentence. Turned her head to the side.

"Elle? You still there?"

"I'm here," she whispered. "Sounds like I may not be alone. I think I heard footsteps sliding across the dirt."

"Have you seen anybody out there running on the trail?"

"Not a single soul."

She pulled the phone away from her ear.

Silence.

"I don't hear anything now. Maybe it was just my—"

Bam!

Stinging pain hit the side of Elle's face. She toppled over onto her side.

A blurry figure dressed in all black hovered over her. She screamed.

"Elle?" Todd yelled. *"Elle!* What's going on?"

Her phone was down by her side. But she could still hear his voice.

"Todd! I'm being atta—"

Slap!

The shadowy figure whacked her across the face again, then kicked the flashlight from her hand.

A rock came crashing down toward her chest. Elle rolled over right before it made contact. The stone hit the dirt instead, leaving a deep dent.

Elle grabbed hold of the tulip tree trunk, scrambling to her knees. Jagged bark scraped her palms as she struggled to stand.

She made it onto her feet. But a kick to the stomach knocked her back down.

Elle's body hit the dirt hard. Her whole left side went numb.

The attacker pounced. Black leather gloves went straight for her neck.

"Get away from me!" Elle screamed, reaching up and grabbing hold of the attacker's black ski mask.

The assailant grabbed her wrists and pinned them to the ground. Steely brown eyes glared down at Elle.

She squinted. Peered into them. Those eyes looked familiar.

"Who are you?" she grunted, writhing about to free herself. "Who are you!"

Silence.

"Somebody help me!" Elle screamed.

Her pleas echoed into the distance, then faded. The trail was empty. She was left to fend for herself.

You should've brought a weapon. Why didn't you bring a weapon?

Elle knew why. She hadn't expected to be assaulted. All of their suspects were accounted for. All except…

Bryce!

Elle kicked her leg high in the air, attempting to knee him in the groin. He jumped up, avoiding the impact before slamming back down on top of her.

She cried out in agony.

"Bryce! I know it's you. Get off me!"

He didn't budge. She choked underneath the weight of his body.

"Now I know why you didn't show up to the station," she wheezed. "You were too busy following me! You won't get away with this. I was just on the phone with Todd. He knows where I am. And he heard you attacking me! He'll be here any minute—"

"You'll be dead and we'll both be gone before he gets here…"

Elle cringed at the sound of his raspy, whimpering voice. The same voice that left the messages on her phone.

"You sound disgusting, you…you *maniac*. What is that, your serial killer voice? Because that's what you are. A serial killer!"

"Shut up!"

Whack!

Bryce punched Elle square in the jaw. She screamed out in agony. Her entire face throbbed as if it had been shattered into a thousand pieces.

She lay there, unable to move. Bryce pounced once again, going straight for her neck.

His clammy leather gloves clung to her throat. Elle grabbed his wrists and pulled. Bryce's hands didn't budge.

"Please," she gasped. "Stop…*please!*"

His grip tightened.

She pulled harder, gagging from the pressure of his suffocating grasp.

Her eyes bulged, then glazed over.

"Die," he wheezed. "That's it. Die!"

Elle's eyelids lowered while her heart raced. She

struggled to take in thin streams of air. Oxygen evaded her lungs.

Her limbs began to convulse. Bryce squeezed her legs between his knees, showing no mercy.

"Aww, look at that," he hissed. "Two best friends, dying the same death. Is your throat closing up, just like Taylor's? Are you losing consciousness? Is your windpipe getting crushed?"

Elle felt herself slipping away.

A man's voice rippled through the mountain air.

"Stop!"

Despite being half-conscious, Elle felt her eyes fill with tears of relief.

Todd!

Bryce's grip let up.

Elle took advantage of the reprieve. Made a feeble attempt to push him off her. But she was too weak.

"Get away from her!" Todd yelled as his voice drew nearer.

Bryce didn't budge.

"Get up! *Now!*"

Pounding footsteps approached, then skid across the dirt path.

Elle blinked rapidly, straining to clear her blurred vision.

Her dilated eyes gradually regained focus. And then...

Confusion hit.

Bryce stood over Elle. *And* her attacker.

Who is this?

"Get up!" Bryce yelled, pulling the assailant by the arm.

The assailant didn't budge.

Bryce kicked the attacker in the back.

That did the trick. Elle was finally freed.

She rolled over, choking on a rush of air.

Bryce pounced on the assailant. A tussle ensued. Punches were thrown amid screams and grunts.

Elle pulled herself up, watching as Bryce got the upper hand.

He grabbed hold of the ski mask and tore it off. Shined his flashlight in the assailant's face.

Elle recoiled, falling back against the tulip tree.

She screamed, nearly fainting from shock.

It was Audrey.

"It's over, Audrey," Bryce said. "You're done. Do you hear me? *Done!*"

"No!" Audrey screamed.

She shoved Bryce to the ground, then went straight for Elle. Took hold of her throat and squeezed. Her twisted expression filled with rage.

"Die, bitch. Die!"

Elle gasped, clawing at Audrey's arms. The deranged woman refused to let up.

Bang!

A gunshot blasted overhead.

"Everyone on your knees with your hands up!"

Todd! For real this time!

Audrey squeezed harder despite the warning shot. She was possessed, determined to crush the life out of Elle.

Todd rushed the group.

Audrey released Elle and scrambled to her feet, attempting to make a run for it.

Todd grabbed her by the collar and pulled her back, holding his gun to her head.

"If you do not stand down, I will shoot."

Audrey finally relented, sobbing as she fell to her knees, and buried her face in the dirt.

"Just kill me now," she cried. "Just kill me now!"

Todd placed her in handcuffs. "Audrey Bingham, you are under arrest. You have the right to remain silent. Anything you say can and will be used against you in a court of law..."

Bryce rushed over and helped Elle to her feet.

"I am so sorry," he said. "Are you okay?"

She ran her hand down her throat, wincing in pain. "I—I think so..."

"Elle," Todd said, "I've got backup and an ambulance on the way. Hang in there. You'll be fine. Bryce, can you help get her down to the bottom of the trail while I escort Ms. Bingham?"

"Sure thing."

Elle and Todd shared a long glance. In it was everything they felt. The relief, the gratitude, the resolve. But most importantly, the love.

Chapter Twenty-Six

Todd sat next to Sheriff Glover inside the station's tiny interrogation room. Audrey was seated across from them, slumped down in her gray metal chair with her arms folded tightly over her chest.

A fluorescent white lightbulb flickered overhead, buzzing loudly. Todd tuned it out while focusing on Audrey, who was staring down at the dingy beige carpet with her lips puckered smugly. She hadn't spoken a word since they'd left the hiking trail.

Todd turned on his tape recorder while Sheriff Glover cracked open his notebook. "There's a lot to unpack here, Audrey," Todd began. "Where should we start?"

She snorted loudly and shrugged her shoulders. "F it. What've I got to lose? I might as well tell you everything. Then you'll realize that I'm the victim in all of this. Not Harper. Not Taylor. Not Sara. *Me*."

"Oh," Todd said, leaning into the table, "so you're admitting to killing Harper and Sara, too?"

Audrey turned away and bit her cheek.

"Got a little ahead of yourself there, didn't you?" Sheriff Glover asked. "Said too much. I'll tell you what.

Since you wanna to tell us everything, why don't we start here—why did you kill Harper Mitchell?"

She sat straight up and looked the sheriff directly in the eyes. "Because I was having an affair with her husband."

Todd forced his poker face to remain intact as he remembered Keaton mentioning his extramarital affairs.

"So you killed her?" the sheriff probed. "Over an affair?"

"Yes."

Her boldness almost knocked Todd out of his chair. "Why?"

"Because her husband was miserable in that marriage. Keaton was trying to part ways amicably, but she refused to sign the divorce papers. The greedy bitch kept begging for a bigger settlement. Then she really pissed me off when she stole a scarf that belonged to his mother. So, that's when I stepped in."

"Exactly how did you step in?" Todd asked.

"By getting the scarf back. But not before I strangled her to death with it."

Todd went cold. Sitting face-to-face in front of a psychopath was bone-chilling, to say the least.

"Wow," Sheriff Glover uttered while wiping sweat from his brow. "Never in my thirty-plus years…"

"Look," Audrey said, "I was just trying to fix the situation. You know, do the right thing. For Keaton. For *us*. But then…"

"Then what?" Todd asked.

The veins in Audrey's neck pulsated. "He refused to marry me. And I found out that he was seeing other women. I wanted to kill him, too. Then I met Bryce. We just…we clicked. He's the reason why I moved to Bradford. He got me the job at the car dealership, helped me find a home near his."

Todd's hands curled into tight fists underneath the table. Bryce had conveniently left all of that out when they'd spoken.

Deal with him later. Focus on Audrey's confession for now.

"Deputy Jacobson," Sheriff Glover said, "I know this case is personal for you. Are you sure you're okay listening to this?"

"Absolutely, sir. I'm here to get justice for my sister. I want to see investigation all the way through." He turned to Audrey. "Now, why did you kill Taylor? Because Bryce wouldn't divorce her?"

"Nope," she said, cocking her head to the side. "That's not the reason at all. Those two were in financial ruin. A divorce would've put Bryce further in the hole. Getting rid of Taylor meant he could cash in on her life insurance policy, get out of debt, and live happily ever after with me. But then Sara and Elle started interfering in my plan. So I tried to get rid of them before they figured me out. Unfortunately, I was only fifty percent successful."

"And look at what ended up happening," Todd said. "The very man you killed for helped assist in your arrest."

The smirk on Audrey's face fell.

"How did Bryce know you were at River Birch Park this evening?" Sheriff Glover asked. "Did you tell him what you were planning to do?"

One lone tear trickled down Audrey's cheek. It was the first time she'd shown any sign of emotion.

"No," she admitted. "He didn't. And that's where I

messed up. We were both at the dealership, and I knew he was supposed to meet Deputy Jacobson at the station for questioning. The walls were closing in on me. So I snuck out of work in one of the dealership's cars and went to Elle's house. Followed her to the hiking trail. But I forgot that some of the cars on the lot have trackers. Bryce must've realized I was gone and traced the whereabouts of the vehicle."

There was a knock at the door.

"Come in!" Sheriff Glover called out.

Deputy Cross stuck his head inside. "Excuse the interruption. Sheriff, can I please speak with you for a second?"

Todd and Audrey glared at one another silently while the two men shared a brief exchange.

"Good work," Sheriff Glover told Deputy Cross. "Thanks for the update."

He closed the door and took a seat. "We found the black pickup truck you'd been driving around town at a private garage over on Astor Street. You were renting the space from a woman named Mrs. Wilson?"

Audrey dropped her head down onto the table.

"The description matches the one that Elle Scott had given us. And the tire tracks match those that were photographed at Everest Forest Preserve the day you crashed into Ms. Scott's car." The sheriff turned to Todd. "Oh, and the *deputies* found Elle's laptop wrapped in a blanket inside the truck's cargo bed."

"Good. She'll be glad to have that back."

Sheriff Glover opened a file that Deputy Cross had given him and slid it across the table. "I'm not done yet. Look at what's behind door number three. Your fingerprints match the one that was found at the Scotts' residence."

Todd tapped Audrey's shoulder. She sat back up. He stared into her cold, vacant eyes.

"Were you the one behind all of the stalking? And the threatening messages? The shooting at my house?"

She nodded.

"Audrey, do you understand how many lives you've ruined?"

Her mouth opened and closed several times as she pulled at the handcuffs binding her wrists. "I just—I just wanted someone to love me…"

Sheriff Glover stood and walked around the table. "We've heard enough. Deputy Jacobson, I'm sure you wanna get to the hospital and check on Elle. I'll take over from here."

"Thank you, sir."

The sheriff stopped Todd before he left the room. "Listen," he whispered, "I owe you an apology. I should've listened to you on this one and reopened Taylor's case a long time ago. You single-handedly got it solved. Excellent job. I'm proud of you."

"Thank you, sir. Elle was a huge help in all of this, too. I couldn't have done it without her."

"I'll be sure to share those same sentiments with her as well. Oh, and I'll be looking into the shoddy investigation into Harper Mitchell's death, too. As for you, let's talk promotion once the dust settles."

"That would be great, Sheriff. Thanks again."

Todd ran to his desk and grabbed his keys, his mind now focused solely on Elle.

On the way out the door, his cell phone buzzed. It was a text message from her.

The doc just examined me. I'm fine. No serious injuries. Just a little bruising and soreness. I'll be released tonight.

Relief almost knocked Todd to the floor.

I am so glad to hear that, he wrote back. I'm on my way there now. See you soon. Love you.

Love you, too.

Chapter Twenty-Seven

"Merry Christmas, Elle."

"Merry Christmas, Todd."

The pair clinked their glasses together and took sips of strawberry Bellini as they sat underneath Todd's Christmas tree.

"I've got another gift for you," he said.

"But you already gave me the most beautiful silk robe. Why are you spoiling me like this?"

"No, *I'm* the spoiled one. Those fancy cigars you gifted me are hard to come by. But hold on. This is a different type of present. You know that twig you recovered from the crime scene?"

"I do."

"The forensics came back on it."

Elle propped herself up onto her elbow. "And? What were the results?"

"Taylor's DNA was present. So was Audrey's."

"Yes!" Elle exclaimed. "Time to update my business card. Which sounds better? Elle Scott, crime scene investigator? Or Elle Scott, forensic investigator? Or—"

"Hold on, hold on, let's not get ahead of ourselves," Todd said with an amorous chuckle. "You do deserve your accolades, though. I don't know how law enforcement could've missed that twig time and time again. Leave it to my eagle-eyed girl to find it."

He ran his finger across her cheek.

"I definitely think I should be rewarded," she murmured.

"Oh, you should absolutely be rewarded."

Todd wrapped his arm around the small of her back and pulled her close.

"There's something I've been wanting to say to you in person as opposed to text," he said.

"Oh, really? What's that?"

"I love you."

Elle's breath caught in her throat. Her lips parted.

Before she could speak, Todd continued.

"I knew that I loved you the minute you arrived back in Bradford. You've been here by my side during the hardest time of my life. You rode with me nonstop, determined to help solve Taylor's murder. Through the ups, the downs, the triumphs and the disappointments, your support never wavered."

"Thank you, Todd. I can say the same for you. I am so proud of the work we've done together. Partnering with you has proven one thing to be true."

"Which is?"

"That I lo—"

Todd pressed his lips against hers before she could finish.

Elle melted into his kiss, growing dizzy from the joy swirling inside of her.

Several moments passed before they pulled away from each other. And when they did, Elle responded with a breathless "I love you, too."

* * * * *

COMING NEXT MONTH FROM

HARLEQUIN
INTRIGUE

#2115 LAWMAN TO THE CORE
The Law in Lubbock County • by Delores Fossen
When an intruder attacks Hallie Stanton and tries to kidnap the baby she's adopting, her former boss, ATF agent Nick Brodie, is on the case. But will his feelings for Hallie and her son hinder his ability to shut down a dangerous black market baby ring?

#2116 DOCKSIDE DANGER
The Lost Girls • by Carol Ericson
To protect his latest discovery, FBI agent Tim Ruskin needs LAPD homicide detective Jane Falco off the case. But when intel from the FBI brass clashes with the clues Jane is uncovering, Tim's instincts tell him to put his trust in the determined cop, peril be damned.

#2117 MOUNTAIN TERROR
Eagle Mountain Search and Rescue • by Cindi Myers
A series of bombings have rocked Eagle Mountain, and Deni Traynor's missing father may be the culprit. SAR volunteer Ryan Welch will help the vulnerable schoolteacher unearth the truth. But will the partnership lead them to their target...or something more sinister?

#2118 BRICKELL AVENUE AMBUSH
South Beach Security • by Caridad Piñeiro
Mariela Hernandez has a target on her back, thanks to her abusive ex-husband's latest plot. Teaming up with Ricky Gonzalez and his family's private security firm is her only chance at survival. With bullets flying, Ricky will risk it all to be the hero Mariela needs.

#2119 DARK WATER DISAPPEARANCE
West Investigations • by K.D. Richards
Detective Terrence Sutton is desperate to locate his missing sister—one of three women who recently disappeared from Carling Lake. The only connection to the crimes? A run-down mansion and Nikki King, the woman Terrence loved years ago and who's now back in town...

#2120 WHAT IS HIDDEN
by Janice Kay Johnson
Jo Summerlin's job at her stepfather's spectacular limestone cavern is thrown into chaos when she and former navy SEAL Alan Burke discover a pile of bones and a screaming stranger. Have they infiltrated a serial killer's perfect hiding place?

YOU CAN FIND MORE INFORMATION ON UPCOMING HARLEQUIN TITLES, FREE EXCERPTS AND MORE AT HARLEQUIN.COM.

HICNM1122

HARLEQUIN
PLUS

Announcing a **BRAND-NEW** multimedia subscription service for romance fans like you!

Read, Watch and Play.

Experience the easiest way to get the romance content you crave.

Start your **FREE 7 DAY TRIAL** at <u>www.harlequinplus.com/freetrial</u>.